THE MAN WHO HATED HALLOWEEN

DAVID WHITTAKER

ALSO BY DAVID WHITTAKER

QUINTIN MORRIESON

Cover Design By: Edwin Harris, Jr.

First printing: 2018
ISBN: 9780578210797

Published by:
EC Publishing
Richton Park, Illinois 60471
Eddydynamite14@gmail.com
(708)334-3893

The New Three Stars (N.T.S.) Edward, Benji and Michael are foster brothers in their first year of Jr. High. Edward is very bossy to his two foster brothers Benji and Michael. Edward is the boss of the three, often making the decisions on what they should do or not do. Benji loves to rap while Michael wants to be a basketball player in the NBA when he grows up. On the day of Halloween they were standing by their lockers looking at all the costumes people wore to school. They decided not to wear their costumes to school, but were still planning on going trick or treating that night. They laughed at some of the costumes they saw. Edwin, one of their friends at the school, walked up to their locker wearing a long trench coat with a cigar.

"What's up guys, it's me Edwin," he said.

"What's up Edwin?" they asked him.

"What's up guys?"

"What's up Edwin?"

"What's up guys, you know what."

"What?"

"You know what."

"What?"

"You know what"

"What?"

"I'm gonna set a record for how much candy I get tonight."

"We're gonna have to break it," Michael said.

"We're gonna get so much candy our bags are gonna break," Edward added.

"That's happened to me before," Edwin said.

"Who are you supposed to be, a business man?"

"No, Edwin is in the trench coat mafia," Benji said.

"You guys never saw Columbo before?" Edwin asked.

"Oh that's who you are."

"Is that cigar real?" Michael asked.

"No, you know they wouldn't let me come in school with a

real cigar. Mrs. Robinson already checked to see if it was real or not. Why didn't you guys dress up?" Edwin asked.

"We're saving that for tonight."

"What are you guys gonna be?"

"I'm gonna be a wolf," Edward said.

"Yeah Edwin he doesn't have to wear no mask for that, ha, ha, ha," Benji laughed as Edward's face turned mean. Edward takes Edwin's book out of his hands and crushes Benji's nose in between the book. He hands the book back to Edwin as Benji massages his nose.

"What about you two? " Edwin asked.

"I'm gonna be a Skeleton."

"And I'm gonna be a vampire," Michael said. He opened up his mouth to show Edwin his fangs.

"Well I'll see you guys later," Edwin said, before walking away from their locker. They see Brenda, the captain of the cheerleading team. She was dressed up as Glinda, the Good Witch of the North from the Wizard of Oz. She had a fake pumpkin on her arm.

"Even though you guys are totally not wearing costumes I know you are like going trick or treating tonight so I'm gonna give you each some candy," Brenda said.

"Thank you," they all said. They reached into her fake pumpkin and got candy out.

"Well I may see you trick or treating later, kisses." She walked away from their locker.

"Wow, we already have some candy and we ain't even been trick or treating yet," Benji said.

"Speaking of candy, look," Michael said, as he pointed to one of the girls dressed as a princess. Her name was Candy, she was an eighth grader.

"Man I want some candy."

"And I want some Benji, but I don't date 6th graders," Candy said, as she smiled at him.

"Well when I'm in 8th grade I'll be able to date you."

"No you won't, Candy's gonna be a sophomore in high school."

"What about when you're out of school?"

"Yeah, we can get married then baby." She smiled at Benji. All of them looked at her as she walked away.

"I wouldn't mind having candy," Edward said.

"I want candy," Michael said. He took out a lollipop that was in his pocket. "Now I have it."

"You got it alright." Edward pushes Michael's hand into his head which breaks his lollipop.

"You're a candy breaker Edward, why you." Michael picked up a huge dictionary that was in their locker.

"Wait Michael no!" He threw the dictionary at Edward, but he ducked down. It hit a student that was wearing a hockey mask.

"Naaaw!" they all said.

"You idiot you just hit Jason Voorhees," Benji said.

"What is he doing out of Crystal Lake?" Michael asked.

"I don't know, but he's coming this way," Edward said. They turned, in an attempt to run, but the hallway was too packed for them to go anywhere. When they turned around the man wearing the hockey mask was standing in front of them. "Look Jason, we're sorry man, we didn't mean to do it."

"Yeah, I was trying to hit this idiot." Michael pointed at Edward.

"Who you calling an idiot?" Edward smacked Michael. The man in the hockey mask began lifting it off. "No don't!"

"Yeah he has a face scarier than yours Edward," Benji said. Edward elbowed him in the head. "Oh." When his mask was completely off they were surprised to see Travis, who everyone called T Money.

"Oh T Money it's only you," Michael said.

"Yeah who did you think it was, the real Jason, it's Halloween you stupid fools!," he said.

"We keep forgetting that it's Halloween," Edward said.

"You guys are slow, how could you forget? Everyone's in costumes except you fools!"

"I forgot, whenever I see that Jason mask I think of Jason, we thought you were the real one."

"Jason? Jason? Jason doesn't exist!"

"It's no explaining to them, they don't understand anything," one of the girls passing in the hallway said.

"Who are you supposed to be?" Benji asked.

"See." She rolled her eyes. "What do you think I'm supposed to be?"

"If we knew we wouldn't ask." Edward hit Benji in his head.

"It's something to do with a church."

"Preachers don't dress like that," Michael said, pointing to her.

"Who said I was a preacher?"

"Well I just said it, ha, ha, ha, ha, yeah, yeah, I sure did." Edward pulled him by his ear and then smacked him in his forehead.

"Whatever you are it's a terrible wardrobe," Edward said.

"At least I dressed up for Halloween," she said.

"I give up, what are you?" Benji asked.

"I'm a nun."

"What's that?" Michael asked.

"That's one of those people that harass you at your house," Edward said.

"Yeah?" Benji asked.

"Yeah they knock on your door with Bibles and smiles."

"No you idiots not Jehovah witness, a nun, I'm a nun!," she said adamantly

"We must've never saw one before."

"Well now you have." She walked away from them.

"Look out guys, so what are you gonna be for Halloween?" Travis asked them.

"A Skeleton, a wolf and a vampire," Edward told him.

"My Skeleton costume is tight," Benji said.

"Why didn't you wear it?" Travis asked.

"I'm saving it for trick or treating."

"Last year we ruined our costumes by wearing them to school," Edward said.

"Yeah, we didn't wanna do that two years in a row."

"Last year we had to make a quick costume run," Michael

said.

"Yeah, a lot of people thought we were dressed up as gay people."

"What were you guys wearing?" Travis asked.

"We were dressed up like the village people."

"Oh, well I may see you guys later when I'm out doing my thang."

"Alright Travis," Edward said.

CHAPTER 2

The N.T.S. hear The Phantom of the Opera music playing on the intercom.

"Ha, ha, ha students this is Principal Jones and you now have 6 minutes to get to class," he said. "Ha, ha, ha, ha, ha, ha, ha, ha, ha.........6 minutes."

"Wow, that was pretty spooky," Michael said.

"Yeah, it's a lot better than those bell sounds we usually hear," Benji said.

"Let's go," Edward said. They walk to their classes. Edward and Michael were in the same first period class. When they got to Mrs. Buechler's class she was dressed up like a chicken.

"Buck, buck, bawk!," she said playfully. The Phantom of the Opera music played over the intercom system again.

"All students should now be in their class, ha, ha, ha, ha, ha," Principal Jones said.

"He's in a good mood today."

"Well it is Halloween," one of the students in her class who was dressed like a Greek god said.

"I wonder what he's dressed up as," Edward said.

"I haven't seen Principal Jones yet, what a sinister laugh though," Mrs. Buechler said. Once everyone was seated Mrs. Buechler began the lesson. "Does anyone know how Halloween started?" No one in the class raised their hand. "Anyone? Does anyone have the answer?" The class still didn't respond. "O.k. I will tell you. It happened a long, long time ago. In the 1800's it is not known how they got on Earth, but demons and all of the other evil creatures of the night walked the Earth one night trying to destroy it. A team full of holy men fought against the demonic forces vowing to defeat them at all cost, even if they died in doing so." A student wearing a Pippi Longstocking costume raised her hand. Mrs. Buechler pointed to her. "Mandy."

"Did they win?" Mandy asked.

"Yes but do you know how they won?" The class was silent. "Can anyone guess how they defeated them?" A student wearing a sailor outfit raised his hand. She pointed to him.

"They threw holy water on them," the student wearing the sailor outfit said.

"Good guess, but no. Anyone else wanna answer?" The class didn't respond. "They dressed up like demons and other creatures of the night and they were able to trick them and send them back to where they came from and thus the Earth realm was saved from total evil. This happened on October 31, well that's what the legend says, but all legends have some truth behind them. Michael raised his hand. "Yes Michael."

"Where did the jack-o-lanterns come from?" Michael asked.

"According to the legend the night those creatures tried to take over the Earth and destroy it they put a blackout over the Earth. No moon, no stars, just pitch black and dark." When she saw Edward was raising his hand she pointed to him.

"What about street lights?" Edward asked.

"The darkness caused those to stop working, a full out blackout." Many of the students in the class gasped. Some of the students in the class felt scared listening to her.

"That would be pretty scary Mrs. Buechler," Tim said, who was dressed in a hooded white robe.

"Yes it would be, but to answer Michael's original question class, the holy men carved pumpkins and put candles inside so they could see where they were going while they stopped the evil creatures and that's how we got the jack-o-lantern. So according to the legend every time we dress up on Halloween we are remembering the holy men who saved the Earth from total destruction." A little girl dressed with white makeup, a black witch's hat, a black shirt with matching pants and a red coat raised her hand. "Yes Jenny Maple."

"Why do we go to the house and say trick or treat and then get candy?" Jenny Maple asked.

"That's a good question Jenny Maple, one of the reasons historians say this is done is because of the wording. Trick or treat, meaning if you are not given candy you could do something mean to the persons house, almost like a trick so that's why candy is given to stop that from happening. Another reason I read was for prayer for the lost souls. Every time a person would give the trick or treater food the trick or treater would say god bless you and then pray for all the lost souls and those stuck in purgatory." Michael raised his hand. "Yes Michael."

"What's purgatory?" Michael asked.

"After a person dies they're not in heaven nor hell." Michael gulped, he wished he hadn't asked. "The last reason I read and this is what I believe is the night all that evil was unleashed on the Earth the demons were coming to people's doors and snatching their souls. Since we are not demons we don't ask for souls when we come to people's doors on Halloween, we have our own souls. All we ask for is candy." The class was so silent you could hear a pen drop from the hallway. Michael raised his hand again. "Yes Michael."

"I believe that one too." For the rest of the class period they talked about Halloween characters and Mrs. Buechler went around the room and asked all her students what their favorite horror movie was and their favorite horror icon. Although the class was young she knew some of the parents let them watch things they probably shouldn't. Michael had a day dream that he, Benji and Edward were running from Frankenstein's monster, the Wolfman and Dracula. When he woke up out of the day dream he was a little disoriented. He realized he was still in class. They heard the Halloween movie score over the intercom. They knew it was time to go to their 2nd period class.

"Hold on before you leave you must take some candy." Mrs. Buechler ran to the door in order to give it to everyone in her class as they left.

"I hope she didn't poison it," Michael said quietly to Edward.

"I heard that." All of the students got candy out of Mrs. Buechler's pumpkin before they exited her class room. When Edward and Michael walked into the hallway they met up with Benji. They saw a clown with long shoes walking in the hallway.

"Nice costume."

"Thank you," the clown said. He stopped and gave them some candy.

"That's a tall clown," Benji said.

"I think it's one of the teachers," Edward said.

"Yeah, I don't think we have anybody that tall at our school." They saw The Phantom of the opera. He took off his mask in front of them.

"Oh it's you Principal Jones." They were all very surprised.

"No wonder the first music you played was Phantom of the opera," Michael said.

"Yes, I'm the Phantom, ha, ha, ha, ha," Principal Jones laughed.

"What's so funny?" Edward asked.

"I don't know, I guess I'm just having a phantom moment. Huh, huuuh, huuuh, o.k. it's done." Principal Jones walked away. The N.T.S see a cowboy walking in the hallway.

"Howdy," Michael said.

"Howdy partner," the cowboy said. He walked away. A girl with mouse ears was walking by. All three of them immediately took a liking to the girl.

"Aye beautiful who are you supposed to be Mickey Mouse?" Edward asked.

"No, I'm Minnie Mouse," the girl said. "See the blush on my face?" She pointed at the makeup on her cheeks.

"Well you're the prettiest mouse I've ever seen," Michael said.

"Thank you."

"Are you an 8th grader?" Benji asked.

"No, I'm in 7th grade."

"What's your name sweetheart?" Edward asked.

"Alexandria, but all my friends call me A.J. What are your names?"

"I'm Edward."

"I'm Benji."

"I'm Michael."

"Nice to make your acquaintance." She slightly bowed.

"Why didn't you guys dress up?"

"We're saving our costumes for tonight."

"Oh you guys are going trick or treating?"

"Yeah," Edward said.

"You guys could have worn them for a sneak peak."

"Last year we got into a fight and our costumes were ruined."

"Not too many fights happen at Hughes, especially on Halloween."

"We were wearing the same costumes as three other students," Benji said.

"Yeah and they jumped us," Michael said.

"That's pretty bad, well this year hopefully I don't get jumped, I'm going alone," A.J. said.

"You shouldn't go alone," Edward said.

"Yeah, Edward's right, you should go with us," Benji said.

"Where do you stay?" Michael asked.

"Belmont Park," A.J. said.

"You stay close to us. You don't have to go trick or treating by yourself," Edward said.

"Yeah we can go with you," Benji said.

"Or vice versa," Michael added.

"Thanks guys, here's my number," A.J. said as she go out a piece of paper from her book bag and wrote down her number. She handed it to Edward. "What time are you guys talking about going?" The N.T.S. look at each other.

"Uh I don't know, maybe like 5, 5:30," Edward said.

"That's a good time, let me have yours."

"Benji." Benji tore out a piece of paper from his notebook and wrote down his number. He handed it to A.J.

"Well I'll see you guys later."

"Bye," they said. She walked away.

CHAPTER 3

The N.T.S. heard a familiar tune. Benji smiled, Michael looked confused and Edward nodded to the tune.

"Wait that's that," Edward started.

"It's Superman!" Michael said, pointing to the student dressed as Superman for Halloween.

"You're one of my favorite super heroes for Halloween," Edward told the student.

"I'm not just Superman," the student said. He ran into the bathroom and came out in less than a minute with a suit and glasses on. "I'm Clark Kent too." Edward, Benji and Michael laughed.

"That's a good disguise buddy."

"But shhh don't tell anybody." Edward nodded his head. "I don't want Lois finding out."

"Oh Clark there you are," a girl wearing a black skirt said. They could tell she was dressed up for Halloween.

"Who are you supposed to be?" Benji asked the girl.

"Lois Lane." The two students kissed on the lips.

"I don't remember Clark getting that much love."

"You look good with glasses Mark."

"Thanks baby," Mark said before kissing her again.

"Do you guys mind?" a man with a camera asked.

"No." They pose and then he snaps a picture of them.

"Let me take one more."

"Maybe we should have worn our costumes," Benji said to Edward.

"Yeah, I didn't know they were gonna be taking pictures," Edward said.

"Where do you think they're gonna put them once they're developed?" Michael asked Edward. Edward shrugged his shoulders.

"Maybe in the hallways, I don't know, that's a good question."

The camera man took another picture of the couple dressed up like Lois Lane and Clark Kent. "Aye excuse me where are you gonna hang these pictures after they're developed?"

"We're not gonna hang them, they're going in the year book," the camera man explained.

"Oh. I keep forgetting we get a year book in junior high."

"Yeah I forgot about that too," Benji said.

"I thought yearbooks were only for high school students," Michael said.

"Look." Benji pointed to a girl wearing a pink prom dress with blood on it. On her head she was wearing a crown. "Who are you supposed to be?"

"Carrie," the girl said.

"No, I mean who are you dressed up as?"

"Carrie."

"Not your name, your costume," Michael said.

"Carrie."

"What they mean is what was that costume inspired by?" Edward asked.

"Carrie."

"Do you always talk in 3rd person?" Michael asked.

"Have you guys ever seen the movie Carrie before?"

"Oh that's the movie with the girl with the teleka... teleka...," Edward said.

"Telegram?" Michael asked. The girl rolled her eyes.

"No." Edward smacked Michael in his face.

"Oh, oh."

"Teleka.."

"Telekinesis," the girl said.

"Gesondheid," Benji said. She rolled her eyes again.

"Get out," Edward said before smacking Benji across his face. "Telekinesis, yeah that's the one, that's a scary movie. Great costume." She smiled at Edward.

"Thank you," she said.

"Isn't that a great costume boys?"

"We don't know, we've never seen Carrie before," Michael

said.

"Yeah, it could be a terrible costume, we've never seen the movie to know whether it is a great costume or not," Benji explained as she rolled her eyes once again.

"Have you seen one smack?" Edward asked.

"No what's that movie about?"

"This." Edwards smacks both of them in the face.

"I know you guys can't go trick or treating like that," the girl tells them.

"No we left our costumes at home," Benji said.

"Good that does you here. Why didn't you wear them to school?"

"Do we have to keep telling that story?"

"Shut up!," Edward said. "Last year we got jumped on Halloween."

"So, I don't see the connection," the girl told Edward.

"We were jumped because our costumes were the same as three other guys," Michael explained.

"They didn't take to us too kind that we were wearing the same thing as they were," Edward said.

"That's bad, are you still going trick or treating?" the girl asked.

"Yeah."

"I'll go with you guys." The three of them were delighted. "My boyfriend was supposed to go with me, but now he's my ex-boyfriend."

"Great, now I have a chance," Benji said. She blushed as she looked at Benji smile at her. Edward smacked Benji in the face. She wrote down her number and gave it to Benji.

"Just call me after school and let me know what time you're going."

"O.k. we will. Oh by the way what is your name?"

"Gloria."

"Hereford?"

"No, Gloria Blake." She began to walk away.

"Wait you didn't ask us our names," Edward said. She

stopped walking and turned around to look at them.

"I know your names, Edward, Benji and Michael." They were surprised.

"How did you know?" Benji asked. With a big smile on her face she responded to Benji's question.

"Everybody knows you guys." She walked away.

When they got home Benji turned on the TV. House on Haunted Hill starring Vincent Price was on.

"I don't wanna watch no black and white stuff," Michael complained.

"This is House on Haunted Hill," Benji explained. "This is a classic with Vincent Price."

"I still don't wanna watch it." Michael took the controller and turned the channel. "See Thriller is on, Vincent Price is in this too and I'd rather watch this than the House on Haunted Hill." Benji looked mean at Michael. Michael started doing the Thriller dance as they did it on the television.

"We've seen that a million times and we have it on tape somewhere here." Benji took the controller and changed it back to House on Haunted Hill.

"Aye I wanna watch Thriller." He snatched the controller away from Benji and turned the channel.

"Hey give me that."

"Go get it." Michael threw the controller. When they realized it hit Edward in the head they became worried. After shaking off the hit to his head Edward walks towards them with a mean look on his face.

"You dummies what are you guys doing, trying to break the controller?" Edward asked.

"No, I was watching House on Haunted Hill and he came here and changed the channel," Benji said. Edward looked over at his foster brother.

"Well that was very rude Mike."

"Well I didn't wanna watch House on Haunted Hill, I wanted to watch Thriller," Michael said

"And I wanna watch House on Haunted Hill!," Benji said as

he got directly in Michael's face.

"Thriller."

"House on Haunted Hill."

"Thriller."

"House on Haunted Hill."

"Thriller."

"Guys," Edward said.

"What?" they both answered Edward. He smacked both of them and then turned the channel.

"We're gonna watch Halloween and that's final!"

"Why do we have to watch Halloween?" Benji asked.

"Cause this is what I wanna watch, you got a problem with that?"

"No, not really."

"Plus I'm tired of you guys arguing about it. Besides we have another TV. in our...." Michael and Benji ran to their room, knocking over Edward in the process. When Edward lifted his head off of the ground he could hear them arguing again. "I wish it was time to go trick or treating. That way I wouldn't have to hear those idiots argue, gosh!"

Later on the N.T.S. were putting on their costumes. Edward decided to call Gloria as they were getting ready.

"Hello," a voice answered after three rings.

"Can I please speak to Gloria?" Edward asked.

"Hold on."

"Hello," Gloria said.

"Gloria this is Edward, we're gonna be leaving in a hour. Do you want us to walk your way?"

"No I'll be over there in 20 minutes, just give me the address."

"O.k. it's 22511 Granada Ave. You know how to get here?"

"Yeah."

"O.k., see you shortly."

"Alright." She hung up the phone. Edward called A.J. After one ring someone answered the phone.

"Hello." the voice said. Edward thought it sounded like A.J.

"A.J.?" Edward asked.

"Yes, who is this?"

"This is Edward from school."

"Oh what's up?"

"We're getting ready now."

"O.k. give me about an hour and I'll be over there."

"O.k."

"Bye."

"Bye." Edward put the phone back on the hook. Edward walked into the bathroom where Michael and Benji were getting dressed in their costumes. "Hey chowder brains the girls will be over here soon."

"I wonder what they're gonna be," Michael said.

"Yeah maybe they'll have scarier costumes than us," Benji said. "What do you think they'll be wearing Edward?"

"What do you think they'll be wearing?" Edward asked.

"We don't know, that's why we're asking you."

"Probably the same thing they wore this morning you idiots!" Edward hits both of them in the head with the Listerine mouthwash bottle.

"Sorry Edward, we forgot."

"Well don't ask anymore stupid questions!"

"Aye Edward why can't we just go trick or treating now?" Michael asked.

"Man you guys are asking stupid questions."

"Why?"

"Cause the girls are going with us stup!"

"Oh yeah, I don't remember girls going with us before."

"This is the first time we've went trick or treating with girls. We play our cards right we may have dates for the 6th grade dance in the spring."

"But Edward, it's only two girls," Benji said.

"That means one of us is gonna be the odd man out," Michael said.

"I said if we play our cards right, there's no guarantee of anything at this point," Edward said.

Meanwhile a few blocks over Professor Gibbs, the mad

scientist was testing two of his machines.

"I can't wait until those trick or treaters get here. I will have a surprise for all of them. They will never step foot in this dimension again! Ha, ha, ha, ha, ha, ha, ha," Professor Gibbs laughed.

After an hour had passed the N.T.S hear their door bell ring. They all ran towards the door. By accident Benji and Michael bumped their heads together.

"Spread out, I'll get the door," Edward said. He opened the door and saw A.J. still dressed as Minnie Mouse.

"Hey," She said. Edward had a huge smile on his face.

"Hi, come in." She walked into the house and sat on the couch. Michael walked into the room.

"What's up A.J.?" Michael asked.

"Hey, uhh, uhh," A.J. said, as she tried to remember his name.

"Michael."

"Oh yeah hi Michael." Edward walked away and the doorbell rang again. He went back to the door and opened it..

"Trick or Treat!," the three trick or treaters at the door said.

"Sorry, thought you were someone else," Edward said. He began to shut the door.

"Wait, wait," one of the trick or treaters said. Edward stopped closing the door. " You don't have any candy?"

"No I haven't even been trick or treating myself."

"After you go will you share your candy with us?"

"No." Edward slams the door shut. As soon as he began walking away from the door the doorbell rang again. "Trick or treaters again, I need to post a sign, we don't have candy." Edward turned around and opened the door. "Listen we don't have any candy!" The girl at the door dressed in a bloody prom dress laughed. Edward realized it was Gloria. "Oh Gloria sorry come in." Gloria was still laughing. "Gloria sit down, this is A.J., she's going trick or treating with us too."

"Oh hi," Gloria said to A.J., holding her hand out. They shook hands. "I wanna see your mask, somebody told me you had a wolf mask."

"Ohhhh let me see it," A.J. said.

"Who told you?" Edward asked.

"I won't tell," Gloria said and then laughed. Edward left the room to get his mask.

"Rrrrrr!," the girls heard from behind the couch. They ran off the couch screaming. When they turned around they saw Edward in his wolf mask. He took it off.

"Edward," they complained playfully.

"That was a good one," Gloria said.

"Yeah you had my heart beat racing," A.J. said.

"Don't worry A.J., I'll protect you," Benji said, as he walked into the room wearing his Skeleton costume. The girls got excited and ran up to him.

"Nice Benji, you're having an out of body experience."

"No an out of skin experience," Gloria said. The girls laughed.

"We're missing one." Gloria looked around the room.

"Yeah, Michael, Michael!" Soon both girls were chanting Michael's name as if they were at a sporting event. Michael came out of the room slow, wearing his vampire robe and his false teeth. A.J. and Gloria laughed and then began clapping. "Alright Michael!"

"That's a handsome vampire."

"How come I'm not handsome?" Benji asked A.J.

"Cause you're a Skeleton," A.J. reminded him.

"Yeah how many skeletons do you know that are handsome?" Gloria asked.

"Not that many, but most of them don't look this good," Benji said. Gloria smiled at him.

"You girls ready to go?" Edward asked.

"Yeah," they both said.

"You girls need something to put your candy in?" Michael asked.

"Dang, that's what I forgot," A.J. said.

"Don't worry sweetie, we'll give you one of our pillow cases," Edward said.

"Pillow cases?"

"Yeah that's what we're using, what's wrong with that?"

"Nothing, I'm surprised me and my friends never thought of

that before."

"I've never used that before either," Gloria said. "Whenever I go with my friends we use paper bags and then when they get full we go back home and get some more."

"Or empty them," both girls said simultaneously as they looked at each other and smiled. They began laughing.

"So I assume both of you will need pillow cases?" Edward asked.

"Yeah, I need one too," Gloria said.

"I'll get it," Benji said. He left the room. When he came back he had five pillow cases. He passed them out to everyone in the room.

"I think we are ready," A.J. said.

"Yeah, we are," Edward said.

CHAPTER 4

When the N.T.S., Gloria and A.J. left the house they were all really excited about going trick or treating. It wasn't just the candy they were excited about, but also the tradition.

"This is gonna be fun," A.J. said.

"Yeah, I hope we get so much candy we have to get new pillow cases," Benji said.

"I have a sugar tooth guys, so I hope so."

"I'll eat most of my candy, but I'm gonna give some to my brother," Gloria said.

"Better you than me, ha, ha, ha," Michael laughed. Edward smacked Michael in the face. They walked up to their first house.

"I'll do the honors," A.J. said. She didn't see a doorbell, therefore she knocked on the door. She heard someone walking to the door, thus she moved away from it. When the door was opened they saw an old Caucasian man with small glasses.

"Trick or treat," all of them said. He put candy in their pillow cases. "Thank you." They walked to the next house where Edward rang the doorbell. A high schooler who went to Wilson Classical high school came to the door. "Trick or treat."

"Aye what's up?" he asked them. He put chocolate in their pillow cases.

"Thank you."

Later on when their bags were halfway full they walked up to a scary house. Michael and Benji hesitated to walk across the street.

"Wow that's one spooky looking joint," Edward said to A.J.

"Yeah, I'm glad we have you to protect us," A.J. said as she held on to Edward's arm. Gloria was holding on to his other arm as they got closer to the spooky house. Edward began blushing.

"Well I love all the attention girls, but one of you can hold on to Benji or Mike, right guys." Edward looked over his shoulder and was surprised not to see them. "Where are those Knuckleheads?"

Gloria turned around and pointed behind them. When A.J. and Edward turned around, they saw Michael and Benji standing on the curb of the street, frozen as if their shoes were stapled there. "Why you idiots you! What's the matter with you?"

"Hey we heard you say it first Edward, that joint looks scary," Michael said.

"Hey Benji if you come over here I'll give you a hug," Gloria said.

"That' s o.k., you can come over here and hug me," Benji said.

"I'ma come over there and smack you, what's wrong with you guys, are you cowards?" Edward asked.

"Yes," they both answered.

"If you guys don't' get over here that ghost behind you is gonna possess you," Gloria said.

"Ghost, there's no such thing as.....," Michael said before looking at Benji. They both had terrified looks on their faces. "Ghost, ghost!, naaw." Michael and Benji ran across the street towards the others. A.J. and Gloria moved out of the way when they saw the boys running at a high speed towards them. Benji and Michael knocked over Edward. They were worried about what he might do when they saw they had run him over. "Oh I'm sorry Edward, I'm sorry."

"I'm sorry too," Benji said as they helped him to his feet.

"Wow I was just kidding, didn't know you two would take it that serious," Gloria said.

"She was just kidding." Benji looked at Michael with relief and some confusion on his face. Michael was just relieved.

"Yeah," Edward said. He smacked Benji in his face and then he smacked Michael in his face.

"Come on Edward, we didn't know, what would you do if you saw a ghost?"

"I would run, you didn't see anything and you two morons ran."

"She tricked us," Michael said.

"Well shame on her, let's go," A.J. said. They began walking to the house slowly. Edward and A.J. were holding hands while

Benji and Gloria were holding hands on her left side. Gloria's right hand was being held by Michael, who was also holding three candy bags with his free hand. When they got to the door they all looked at each other.

"Does anyone wanna ring the doorbell?" Edward asked. They all looked around at each other, but no one volunteered to do it. Gloria took a deep breath.

"I'll do it," Gloria said. She pressed the doorbell. No one came to the door.

"See no one's home, let's go," Michael said, as he turned to leave.

"Why you...," Edward said. He smacked Michael in his forehead. They heard the door opening up. It was a very squeaky door.

"Hey Edward, I don't see anybody behind the door."

"It's probably a trick."

"I hate tricks, tricks are for kids," Benji said. Edward kicked Benji right above his ankle. "Ow."

"Cool trick," Gloria said, with a smile on her face.

"But Gloria, what if it ain't no trick?" Michael asked.

"Michael are you a man or a mouse?"

"Mouse." Gloria shook her head as Edward stomped Michael on his foot.

"Ooh, Ooh!" He bent down to rub his foot.

"Enter if you dare!," they heard a voice say from inside the house. The girls were scared.

"Naaaw!," the boys said.

"Too chicken to come in?" They all looked at each other. Gloria grabbed Benji and they ran into the darkness of the house.

"You can go in first," Edward told Michael as he and A.J. stood by the door.

"But Edward I don't wanna go in there," Michael told him.

"You'll be fine, look in there." Edward looked at A.J. and put his finger to his lip, telling her to be quiet. As Michael looked into the house Edward kicked him in his butt, knocking him into the house. Edward and A.J. walked into the house and then the door shut hard.

"Naaaaw," the boys said. The girls screamed. None of them could see anything. They heard a sinister laugh which made them feel worried. They fell through a trap door in the floor. When they landed they saw they were in a huge cage. Many of the kids in their neighborhood were also in big cages. Each cage could hold up to 20 people in it.

"Wait, what is this?" Edward asked.

"Welcome to our hell," one of the boys dressed in a black robe said.

"What's going on?" Benji asked.

"I want out of here!," Gloria demanded.

"Who's responsible for this?" A.J. asked.

"I am," they heard a voice say. When they looked up they saw an older man with glasses and wild blonde hair. He was looking at the N.T.S., Gloria and A.J. "So you made your way to my party."

"If this is a party we didn't get the invitation," Benji said.

"Who are you?" A.J. asked.

"My name is Professor Gibbs," he told her.

"And why did you kidnap us?"

"Kidnap, I didn't kidnap any of you."

"Yeah, keep telling yourself that," Edward said.

"Especially if it makes you feel better," a boy dressed like a cowboy in the cage next to Edward said

"I want my mommy, I wanna go home," a little boy dressed like a train conductor said.

"At least let the little boy go," one of the girls dressed as a ballerina said.

"Yeah, he didn't do anything to you," one of the girls dressed as snow white said.

"He did, you did, all of you did something," Professor Gibbs said.

"We don't even know you," one of the 8th graders dressed like the Terminator said.

"Yeah what did we do?" one of the fourth graders dressed like an injured biker asked.

"All of you celebrated Halloween by knocking on doors

or ringing doorbells and saying trick or treat," Professor Gibbs explained. "I never got a chance to go trick or treating when I was younger and if I couldn't go none of you can go."

"We're not your parents," Michael said.

"Yeah, we're not the ones that didn't take you trick or treating," Edward said.

"If you let us out I'll take you," a little five year old girl dressed like a farmer tells Professor Gibbs.

"Yeah, we'll all take you," a fifteen year old boy dressed like Rocky said.

"Yeah," more of the captives said in agreement.

"Stop!" Professor Gibbs said loudly. "No one is gonna take me anywhere!"

"We don't have to take you anywhere, just take us outta here," Edward said.

"Yeah," the kids in the cages said together.

"Quiet!," Professor Gibbs said. "There are more trick or treaters." Professor Gibbs began to walk away.

"How long are you gonna keep us in here?" asked Michelle, a sixth grader dressed up like a witch.

"Don't worry dear, you guys won't be in here for too much longer. Ha, ha, ha, ha, ha, ha, ha, ha, ha." He walked up the stairs. Although there were many kids trapped in the cages the room became very silent.

"I don't like that laugh," Edward said.

"Me neither," Benji said.

"We gotta get out of here."

"Yeah, but how?" A.J. asked.

"I don't know," Edward said.

"Well you better think of something," Michael said.

"Why do I always have to think of something?"

"We should all think of something," the freshman dressed as a storm trooper told them.

"I got it, I got it," Michael said.

"What?" Edward and Benji asked anxiously.

"We get some gun powder."

"Yes."

"Get a stick of dynamite."

"Yes, yes."

"Light it and blast our way outta here."

"No," Edward and Benji both said, before smacking him on his head. "You dummy you," Edward said.

"Well it was a good idea, now if only we had some dynamite."

"Yeah, and where are we gonna get that from?" Edward asked.

"I don't know, I just thought of the plan, it's your job to execute it."

"I'm gonna execute this." Edward attempted to punch Michael, but he ducked leading him to hit Benji in his face. Benji was partially dazed, but tried to shake it off. "Benji, Benji are you o.k.?"

"Shh here comes some more trick or treaters," the freshman dressed as a storm trooper said. Two girls fell into separate cages. The N.T.S. recognized Brenda, the captain of the 6th grade cheerleading squad.

"Aye look Edward, it's Brenda," Benji said, as he pointed to where she was.

"Yeah, she joined the party," Michael said.

"What is going on, this is like crazy. I wanna know who is responsible for this," Brenda said.

"I am," Professor Gibbs said.

"Who are you and why did you like kidnap me?"

"I am Professor Gibbs and all I need is five more kids, five more."

"Five more and what?"

"Five more and I will let you go." Most of the trick or treaters began screaming with excitement.

"Wait, wait, hold on everybody, hold your applause!," Edward said. The kids in the cages began to get quiet in order to hear what Edward was going to say. "So you said you are gonna let us go, but let us go where?"

"Home?" one of the girls dressed in biker gear asked.

"No far worse than home," Professor Gibbs said. "Wait ,

more trick or treaters, I'll be back." He went up the stairs again as the people in the cages spoke amongst themselves.

"He's gonna let us go, but not home, what is he talking about?" Benji asked.

"I don't know, but we're gonna find out whether we want to or not," Edward said.

"That's what I'm afraid of," the freshman dressed as a storm trooper said.

"What do you think he's gonna do to us?" asked Alexandria, a freshman dressed as Glinda, the good witch of the Wizard of Oz.

"I wish I knew."

CHAPTER 5

The trick or treaters in the cages watch as three more trick or treaters fall from the trap door near the entrance into the basement where all of the cages are. Two boys and one girl this time. Professor Gibbs comes down the stairs with a big smile on his face.

"Two more of you, two more," Professor Gibbs said.

"I'm getting tired of all this, what are you gonna do to us?" Edward asked.

"Yeah, tell us, we deserve to know," the freshman dressed as the storm trooper said. The other captives began screaming out similar thoughts.

"O.k., I will tell you, do you guys see these two machines?" Professor Gibbs asked, referring to the two big machines on the wall. The kids told him they could see both machines. "This first machine is a time machine." All of the kids were quiet and then all of the sudden most of them were laughing. "Quiet! There is nothing funny about this. Do you want me to send you back in time." He pointed directly at Benji. Benji felt his heart beating very fast.

"No," Benji said.

"I could send you back to the caveman days with the dinosaurs so you will be trampled to death by a dinosaur or eaten by a T-Rex."

"That's not funny," one of the 6th graders dressed like Wonder Woman said.

"It would be, but I'm not sending you there. What I have for you is much worse, you can say it's even a nightmare. Ha, ha, ha, ha, ha."

"Professor Gibbs what does the other machine do?" A.J. asked.

"Yeah, like where will it send us?" Brenda asked.

"Yeah what could be worse than being stranded with the dinosaurs?" asked Roscoe, a freshman dressed like Arnold Schwarzenegger in Predator.

"Being sent to a nightmare world where all the demons, all the monsters, all the fictional evil characters you've ever seen on screen exist," Professor Gibbs explained.

"That's not a funny joke," a sixth grader dressed as a policeman said.

"Who said it's a joke?"

"That's impossible, that machine is probably some fancy dryer," Michael said.

"Yeah, that's scientifically impossible," Juan, a freshman dressed as a basketball player said. Many of the kids in the cages agreed.

"Keep telling yourself that, keep reassuring yourself that I'm a crazy old man, we will see when I get two more kids, ha, ha, ha, ha." Professor Gibbs went up the stairs again as the room became silent. Once he was gone the kids in the cages spoke amongst themselves.

"Do you believe him Edward?" A.J. asked. "Could he really be that smart to create a machine that will send us somewhere else?"

"I've heard of parallel dimensions in theory, but this guy is saying he's done it," Edward said.

"I guess we'll find out soon, one way or the other."

"Start praying that he's crazy." Michael and Benji were very nervous.

Outside of Professor Gibbs' house the 8th graders who were dressed up like Clark Kent and Lois Lane were walking towards his house.

"You wanna go there baby?" Mark , who was wearing his Clark Kent suit asked her.

"I don't know it looks kind of spooky honey," the girl dressed as Lois Lane told him. "But I know you wanna go so why not." She smiled at him. They held hands as they walked towards the door to Professor Gibbs' house. "I'll do the honors." She knocked on the door. They saw the door open by itself. They looked at each other and smiled.

"Wow that's pretty spooky."

"I know it is. Should we go in?"

"I guess so."

"Enter if you dare!," they heard a voice say. They laughed as they walked into the house together holding hands. When the door slammed behind them and they could not see anything, they stopped laughing. They heard a sinister laugh and then they screamed when they felt their body falling through the trap door. They fell into the cage with the rest of the trick or treaters who didn't realize the danger they were in when they walked into Professor Gibbs' house. They landed right next to Edward, Benji, Michael, A.J. and Gloria.

"Look Edward, they got Superman," Benji said.

"Yeah, but we're toast, whatever the Professor's planning it's gonna happen now," Edward told Benji.

"Do you really believe that other world stuff Edward?" Gloria asked.

"I don't know what to believe." Professor Gibbs came down the stairs with an evil look on his face.

"It's done, It's done," Professor Gibbs said with excitement in his voice.

"Where are we?" the girl dressed as Lois Lane asked.

"Don't worry about it cause now I'm sending you somewhere else!" He pressed a button on one of the machines. All of the lights in the room went off. Many of the kids screamed, while others cried or asked to be let out. The only thing they could see was the electricity coming from the machine. They heard a loud sound and they felt like they were going to blow away.

"What's happening, I feel like I'm in a tornado," A.J. said.

"Yeah it feels like we're gonna be sucked into a twister," Edward said. The kids continued to scream, cry and some did both as they disappeared from the cages. It was like a wave consumed all of them. Many of the kids closed their eyes while this was happening. When all of the kids reappeared, they were on a dark street. All of them knew they were not close to home. Some of them continued to cry, while others just looked around with fear in their eyes.

"We're not in Kansas anymore," the freshman dressed as a storm trooper said.

"We never were," Michael said looking at Edward. Edward plucked him in his nose.

"Where are we?" a freshman dressed as Storm asked.

"He said he was sending us to a world where all the evil things we read about and see in movies exist," the freshman dressed as a storm trooper said. "But I don't know, it looks deserted."

"There's a sign post," A.J. said, pointing to the street sign.

"It says Elm street," Jennifer, a freshman dressed up like a pink rabbit said. The kids began talking amongst themselves.

"Quiet everyone, quiet!," said the freshman dressed up as a storm trooper. The kids became quiet. "I hear something." All of the kids stayed silent. A little boy dressed like Robin hood walked over to Gloria and held her hand. She looked at him and put her finger to her mouth, signaling for him to be quiet. "I want everyone to quietly start walking that way." The freshman dressed as a storm trooper pointed behind him.

"Why, like what do you see?" Brenda asked.

"No questions, just do what I say if you wanna live."

"But..." A zombie jumped out of the tree and started feeding on Brenda. She screamed as Tamar, a freshman who was dressed up like a wrestler kicked the zombie off of her. Another zombie jumped out of one of the trees and started biting a girl wearing a gown and a crown. Another zombie jumped out of one of the trees and began biting on a 6th grader dressed up like Luke Skywalker. Two others jumped down and began attacking people. The kids looked over and they saw a large number of zombies coming their way.

"Too late, run!" The kids took off running as the zombies came after them.

"Come on," Gloria said, as she picked up the little boy wearing the Robin hood outfit.

"Hold tight on my back o.k.?"

"O.k." the little boy said as he cried. Mark, the boy who was dressed up like Clark Kent kicked and punched a few of the zombies as he was running.

"Mark!," he heard his girlfriend say. He turned around to see where she was.

"Monica!," Mark yelled. A zombie sees him and tries to attack him. He struggled with the zombie, eventually punching him hard enough to knock him to the ground. He ran back to Monica, who was surrounded by three zombies. He screamed really loud in order to get their attention. They tried to chase after him. "Run Monica, run!" He fought them as they attempted to bite him.

"No Mark, I won't leave you." She tried to fight them. They were stunned when they saw one of the zombies arms fly off. They saw two sophomores who were twins, dressed up like pirates fighting the zombies with their swords.

"I'm glad Dad let us borrow his swords," one of the twins told the other.

"Wow, you saved us," Mark told the twins.

"No time for talking, they are everywhere. We've gotta get in doors, but not on Elm street," the other twin said. They continued to walk up the street fighting zombies whenever they had the chance.

Meanwhile the N.T.S., Gloria, A.J. and the freshman dressed as a storm trooper were all catching their breath under a viaduct. Gloria took the little boy off of her back.

"Zombies," Edward said, in between breaths.

"No, fast zombies," Michael said.

"I thought zombies were supposed to be slow," Benji said.

"This isn't the movies anymore," Edward said. Edward looked at the freshman dressed up like a storm trooper, he could tell he was upset. "Aye man, you o.k.?" Everyone looked at him.

"Not really," he said.

"What's wrong?"

"Well besides being chased by zombies, who until tonight I thought were fictional, besides being out of breath and tired, I probably got everyone killed back there."

"You didn't get us killed," Gloria said.

"Yeah, you did a real good job keeping us alive," Edward said.

"But I was trying to help all of us who were in the cages, I wanted to save everyone," said the freshman in the storm trooper outfit.

"You can't save everyone," A.J. said.

"You didn't know those zombies were gonna attack us the

way they did," Edward said.

"Yeah, but I was trying to lead everybody and look what happened," he said with great guilt in his voice.

"This isn't your fault, this is a very sick man's plan," Gloria said.

"Speaking of sick, I feel like I'm gonna be sick," Michael said. He ran from under the viaduct to a huge fountain. It looked like it hadn't been on in years.

"Benji, go with him, but keep quiet," Edward said.

"Why do I always have to go with him?" Benji asked.

"Just do it."

"O.k." Benji went to the fountain where Michael was trying to throw up.

"What did you say your name was?" Edward asked the freshman in the storm trooper outfit.

"Tim O'Connor," he said.

"Tim I'm Edward, this is Gloria, A.J. and the two others are Benji and Michael. I've never seen you before, you weren't at Hughes middle school last year were you?"

"No, I just moved to California this summer."

"Where'd you live before?" Gloria asked. The little boy sat on her lap.

"I stayed in Miami."

"Oh Miami." She couldn't keep the smile off of her face. Gloria and A.J. looked at each other and laughed.

"I wish I were there now."

"I wish I were anywhere but here."

"You said it," Edward said. At the fountain Michael felt sick, but did not throw up.

"How are you?" Benji asked him.

"I don't think I'm gonna throw up," Michael said. Benji noticed Michael was staring into the water.

"What's wrong Mike?"

"Almost looks like, Naaaw." He saw two eyes open, which caused him to move away from the huge fountain. A big splash of water fell on them. When they looked up they saw a short pink creature with sharp teeth.

"Aaaarrhhhhhhhh!," it said.

"Naaaaw," Benji and Michael said.

"I'm outta here," Michael said as the both of them took off running. They ran back towards the viaduct.

"I thought I told those idiots to be....," Edward started to say before he was cut off by Michael.

"We gotta go!"

"Why?"

"Cause of that." Michael pointed to the pink creature as it ran after him and Benji. The girls screamed as they stood up.

"What is that?" Gloria asked.

"Whatever it is it doesn't wanna be friends," Edward said. They began running. They ran across a baseball field as the creature chased after them. They saw baseball equipment on the field, but none of the players, coaches, or people in the stands. When Tim saw the baseball bat he took it and stopped running. The others looked back at him. " Tim what are you doing?"

"Can't run forever," Tim said. He put the baseball bat behind his back. When the pink creature leaped to his feet to attack him he swung the bat at the creatures head. It fell to the ground and did not get back up. They all clapped for him. Tim let go of the bat.

"Tim bring the bat, we may need it again."

"We gotta go now!," A.J. said. They saw more zombies coming their way.

"Let's go," Tim said.

CHAPTER 6

The N.T.S., Gloria, A.J. and Tim ran through the woods behind the baseball field. As they ran they could hear the zombies chasing after them.

"Man, had I known we were gonna get this kind of a workout tonight I would've been a Olympic runner for Halloween," Benji said as he stopped to catch his breath.

"Well you're always the one saying we need to work out more Benji," Edward said.

"Come on we gotta keep moving, they're right behind us," Tim said as he too tried to catch his breath. "What does that sign say?"

"Five miles to Crystal Lake," A.J. said.

"Five miles to Crystal Lake!," they said at the same time.

"Dang, we've covered to much ground to turn back, plus the zombies are behind us. We have to keep going, just watch each other's back," Tim said. "If we do see Jason we'll have to hide."

"Naaw, not a very good strategy," Edward said.

"Hey this bat isn't gonna do anything to him."

"Yeah, you're right." They started walking again. All of them stopped walking when they saw something that terrified them. "It's him," Edward said referring to Jason, he was coming their way.

"Everybody freeze. Don't make any sudden movements, remember he can be tricked." Once he took off the hockey mask all of them were surprised to see Travis.

"Travis," A.J. said.

"You know Travis A.J.?" Benji asked.

"Yeah, everyone knows T Money."

"What's up yall, this is crazy," Travis said.

"Who you telling?" Edward asked.

"We thought you were Jason," Benji said.

"For the 2nd time today," Michael added.

"This time is understandable, we're in a world where he probably does exist, who is this?" Travis asked.

"I'm Tim, I go to Wilson," Tim told him.

"Yeah, I'm Travis." They shook hands.

"Nice to meet you." Travis looked at Gloria.

"I've seen you around the school a lot."

"I'm Gloria, If I had known all of this was gonna happen I would've declined to go trick or treating with them," Gloria said as the little boy asked to be picked up.

"Yeah this is much worse than getting jumped on like we did last year," Edward said.

"I didn't even see you in the cages at Professor Gibbs house," A.J. said to Travis.

"Yeah, I don't think any of us saw you."

"I wonder if Edwin is here," Benji said.

"I didn't see him. I was one of the first to go into the cages," Travis explained.

"What time did you start trick or treating?" Tim asked.

"4:00, I got to Professor Gibbs house about 4:30."

"Who else was in there when you first got captured?" Gloria asked.

"This junior and her ten year old sister, she was talking stuff to Professor Gibbs, but he ignored her."

"Did he talk to you?"

"Not really a conversation, he kept saying I have big plans for you and you will be here for a while and you'll never go home."

"Typical bad guy talk," A.J. said.

"When did the cages start getting packed?" Edward asked.

"Around 5:30 to 6, I didn't see you guys until much later. I saw the wolf mask and was like he must've got Edward, Benji and Michael," Travis said.

"I can't even remember what time we got there. Aye anyone have the time?" Gloria, Tim and Travis all looked at their watches.

"Mines out," Gloria said.

"Mine too," Tim said.

"Ever since we got here my watch hasn't worked," Travis

explained. They heard something in the bushes moving close to them.

"It's time to get going again." They started hearing noises from every direction. The little boy began crying .

"It'll be o.k.," Gloria told him, although she believed the opposite. The noises became more frequent and louder.

"I hate to say this, but I think we're surrounded," Edward said.

"Well it was nice knowing you Gloria," Benji said.

"You too Benji," Gloria said with a worried look on her face.

"It was nice knowing you A.J.," Michael said.

"It was nice knowing you Michael," A.J. said. They saw five zombies jump out of the bushes. Tim turned to look at his new friends with a smirk on his face.

"It's only five, we can take them," Benji said. Five more zombies came out of the bushes. "Uhhhh now we have a problem." The zombies looked at their prey as they decided who to attack first. Tim was holding the bat in a swinging position. They ran towards the visitors from a parallel world trying to bite them. The girls screamed, while the N.T.S closed their eyes. Tim swung his bat while Travis pulled out his fake machete. A huge wolf came to their rescue and killed all of the zombies by biting some while others were eaten. When the people who had closed their eyes opened them they were surprised to see the wolf.

"Nice doggy, nice doggy, be good," Edward said. "T Money you have any doggy biscuits?"

"Sorry Ed, I'm all out," Travis said. The wolf looked like it was going to eat Edward first. To their surprise the wolf turns into a naked man, causing Gloria to smile.

"Gloria don't look at that," A.J. said as she tried to block her vision.

"What, it's out there, how could I not look?" Gloria said with a huge smile on her face. The man put some clothes on that were lying on the ground.

"Sorry for the indecency," the man said.

"I didn't mind." Gloria was still smiling.

"Gloria," A.J. said.

"Wow, what a neat trick," Michael said.

"Who are you?" Tim asked.

"My name is Theodore Rose and I'm what you would refer to as a werewolf," he said. "And these are my friends." They heard the bushes rattle. Two men walked out of the bushes. One of normal height and the other looked like he could've been a wrestler; he was extremely tall and big and his face was pale, as if he hadn't seen any sun in years.

"My name is Count Dracula and this is Frankenstein's monster with me," the man of normal height told them.

"We should of brought some crosses," Benji told Edward.

"No need to be alarmed, we won't hurt you."

"But in our world you and werewolves are evil," Tim said.

"That's what brings me to my first question, where are you actually from, cause it was quite obvious to me and Theodore you were not from here."

"Why do you say that?" T Money asked.

"Well for starters you never walk through Camp Crystal Lake without a gun, secondly most people don't walk through here anyway."

"Why, because of Jason?" Edward asked.

"No, Jason is dead, he's at the bottom of the Lake chained to a rock, but zombies run rapid through these woods, everyone knows."

"Everyone, I haven't seen anyone human here since we've been here, except for us," Tim said.

"Most humans are dead, only a few remain alive. There are demons here, monsters here, dictators, suicidal bombers, sewer creatures, aliens that don't come in peace, you are lucky you're still alive," Theodore said.

"If it wasn't for you we wouldn't be," A.J. said.

"But how did you get here?" Count Dracula asked.

"A crazy professor named...," Tim said before he was cut off by Count Dracula.

"Gibbs?" The travelers from another world all stared at Count Dracula.

"How did you know?"

"There's a Gibbs here too that has claimed for years and years he knows a way out of here. Of course everyone around here thinks he's nuts."

"Where is he now?" A.J. asked.

"He's in a asylum that houses crazy people about 4 hours away from here."

"We always thought he was lying," Theodore said. "He said there was a parallel dimension that existed that was not like the hell we live in now. I assume that's the world you live in."

"You bet it is," Michael said.

"And we can't wait to get back," Benji said.

"But why would you do this for us?" Edward asked.

"Not that we are complaining, it's just that the stories depict you as being a killer and vampires as being evil."

"Some of the legends are true, sunlight, silver, garlic, all those hurt me, but the thirst for blood isn't true, I can go months at a time without needing blood and when I do need it I go to the morgue and steal some instead of killing an innocent human. I don't hunt anymore, if I did I surely would've bit you after Theodore destroyed the zombies," Count Dracula said.

"We just wanna help, nothing else," Theodore said.

"Frankenstein wanna help friends," the monster said. The travelers were surprised he could speak.

"Forgive him, he thinks his name is Frankenstein, even though that is his creators name," Count Dracula said.

"I think we're all surprised he can talk," Gloria said.

"You don't have to take our help, but how long do you expect to stay alive without our help?" Theodore asked.

"We'd love for you to help us," Travis said as he held his hand out for Dracula to shake.

CHAPTER 7

After getting to know one another a little better by exchanging pleasantries and telling short stories to each other, the Count took them to his castle. It looked like a painting from the outside, surrounded by mountains. The travelers got a spooky vibe from the way it looked, but trusted they would be alright. Once they were inside, it was less spooky, but they didn't feel at ease like when they were in their own homes. Dracula went to work making them fake uniforms to wear. He was going to help them get Professor Gibbs out of the asylum. He told them he was the only one that could get them back to their world.

"Now four of you can be doctors, the rest of you have to stay in the van," Dracula said to them.

"What van?" Tim asked.

" I have a huge van the eight of you can ride in."

"You're not going?" A.J. asked.

"It takes 4 hours to get there. They open at 6, by then it will be sunlight and I cannot be in the sun."

"Yeah we know that, so what do you want us to do?" Edward asked.

"Say you are four doctors from Amityville Research. Tell them Count Dracula sent you, Theodore get the papers." Theodore got some papers out of a drawer in the room. He handed them to Dracula. "One of you have to be the lead scientist." Benji smiled and put his hand out. Edward smacked it away.

"I'll be the lead scientist."

"But I wanna be," Michael said.

"You powder brain idiot, this is serious business. I need to be the lead scientist."

"It's always about you Edward, all the time!"

"Aye, I'll be the lead scientist. If anyone objects let them speak now," Tim said. All of Dracula's guests looked at Tim, but said nothing. Dracula handed the papers to Tim.

"I still don't see how this is gonna help us get him out," Travis said.

"Say you are here to study the patient they call Gibbs. You wanna request a transfer to the Dungeon Hall Asylum," Dracula said. "If they reject your transfer get him out anyway you can, but be warned the doctors in there are evil and they will kill you if you don't escape."

"Naaw I'm glad I'm not the leader," Michael said.

"Wimping out already Mike?" Gloria asked with a sarcastic tone.

"Yeah."

"Don't you get it, this may be our only chance home." Her tone was more serious now.

"She's right, it's time to man up," Tim said. He looked at A.J. and Gloria. "And woman up too."

"You ain't gonna send us in there blind are you man?" Travis asked.

"Blind, whatever do you mean Travis?" Count Dracula asked.

"I mean no weapons?"

"Of course, I will walk you to the weapons room now."

"I'm tired," the little boy told Gloria.

"I'll stay here, you can rest on me," Gloria told the little boy. The little boy got into Gloria's arms and rested. "Guys I'm gonna stay here with him."

"I'll stay with you," Benji said. The rest of them left the room. Gloria smiled as she rubbed the young boy. "What's his name?"

"I don't know, he wouldn't tell me."

"Why not?"

"He told me he's not supposed to tell strangers his name." They both laughed.

"You've done a good job with him Gloria."

"Thank you, but I won't feel the job is done until I get him home alive." Benji smiled and then shook his head. "What?"

"I was just thinking last year was crazy, we got jumped on because of our costumes, but this year is wild!"

"No one will believe us."

"I know."

"I will say this Benji Dice, you know how to make a girl's Halloween memorable." They laughed.

"I just hope it's not the last thing we remember," Benji said, causing her smile to vanish.

"Come here." Benji sat down next to her and the little boy that was asleep in her arms. "Don't lose faith, we made it this far, we'll make it, I know we will." Benji put his head down. She lifted it up and gave him a kiss.

"Wow, Wow, Wow!"

"That obviously made you feel better, ha, ha, ha."

"I feel like I can fight Mike Tyson now." Gloria continued to laugh.

"That was just a little peck, just imagine if I would've given you a real kiss."

"I probably would've flown through the roof."

"I think you would of done two back flips and flew through the roof."

In the meantime Edward, Michael, A.J., Tim, Travis, Theodore, Frankenstein's monster and Count Dracula were walking to the weapons room. When they got there they were surprised at how small the room was.

"Doesn't look like we'll find anything in here," Michael said.

"Be patient my friends, looks can be deceiving," Dracula said. Theodore and Dracula pulled out five huge chest boxes. "In these boxes you will find plenty of weapons, but take wisely, you will not be able to sneak all of them with you into the asylum, If the doctors see a lot of weapons on you they will know you are fraudulent."

"You still need weapons for the road, those damn zombies may try to tip over your van," Theodore said. Once they began opening up the chest boxes they were surprised to see all the variety of weapons that were in there.

"Wow, silver bow in arrows, I wonder what you would use this for," Edward said showing it to Count Dracula.

"Be careful with that, you know I am allergic to silver," Count

Dracula said.

"You have a lot of knives," Travis said as he grabbed two.

"There good for stabbing zombies with," Theodore said.

"With all these weapons I'm surprised you and the other vampires didn't rid yourself of all the zombies," Edward said.

"The other vampires don't go by the code," Dracula said.

"What code?" Tim asked as he picked up a butcher knife and a hand gun.

"Vampires never attack humans."

"This world is completely backwards, even with the way you are, you've been nice, but I wanna know is there anything to eat around here?" Travis asked.

"I don't cook, and my cook is out of town, but there are gas stations on the way to the asylum if you wanna stop."

"Where are we gonna put all of these weapons?" Tim asked.

"I have bags here." Dracula pointed to the polypropylene bags that were all empty on the floor next to one of the chest boxes. Edward grabbed one for everyone and gave it to them. After A.J. got her bag she looked at Michael with a serious expression.

"I don't even know if I need this Mike," A.J. said.

"Why?" Michael asked.

"I only got this one gun." She showed him the gun.

"Take more than that, you have to protect yourself sweetheart."

"Well I guess you're right, I just never imagined myself as a gun shooter, or a killer at all."

"Well you never thought Count Dracula existed before tonight."

"Yeah, that's true." He saw a slight smile appear on her face.

"Make sure you guys get bullets too," Tim told everyone in the room that was human. "No good in taking guns if you don't have enough bullets." Frankenstein's monster walked over to Edward.

"Be careful when you go there, Frankenstein doesn't want you to get hurt," the monster said.

"Don't worry big fella, we'll be out of there in no time," Edward said.

"You are all Frankenstein friends." All of the humans in the room smiled at him.

"You're our friend too big guy," Tim said, patting him on his back. Theodore, who had previously left the room as they were picking out weapons returned.

"Who's gonna be the doctors, I found a extra suit, so five can go instead of the four," Theodore said. Edward looked over at Tim and smiled at him. Although he'd just met him, he was already beginning to trust him.

"I think you should pick Tim," Edward said. Tim looked around at all of them.

"I need a man that knows how to fight, T Money you look like you know how to fight," Tim said.

"Yeah, I'll box a zombie to the ground if I have to," Travis said as he swung his arms as if he were in a boxing match.

"I need a man who's a leader in his own right, Edward." He smiled at Tim.

"I won't let you down doctor," Edward said.

"I also need someone who knows you and you know him so I will select Benji, bring some weapons for him too and last I want A.J."

"Me?" A.J. said in total shock Tim chose her.

"Yeah, you are pretty, smart and have more strength than you think you have. I want you with me in the asylum, do you think you can handle that?"

"Yeah, I can handle that." She smiled at him.

"You must wipe off all that paint off your face before you go," Theodore said.

"I forgot about the paint on my face, where's the bathroom?"

"Upstairs," Dracula said.

"Michael will you come with me?"

"To the bathroom, oh boy sure!," Michael said, with noticeable excitement in his voice.

"Michael don't get your hopes up, I just want you to guard the door, this is still a spooky castle."

"It is perfectly safe, but if you feel the need to take Michael with you, then go head," Dracula said.

"Michael come on." They left up the stairs together.

"I need all of you that are doctors to write down your first and last name," Theodore said.

"Why?" Edward asked.

"Your doctor's suits, they have to have your first and last name on it and a picture of you."

"How are you gonna do all of that?"

"Trust me, I have a computer and a printer, that's all I need."

"What about a camera?" Travis asked.

"That's the easiest thing." He pulled out a small camera from his pocket. "Who's first?"

Michael and A.J. were in the bathroom together trying to get the makeup off of her face. Michael had a soap and a rag as he scrubbed A.J.'s cheeks.

"This is one Halloween I'll always remember," A.J. said.

"Me too, we lost all of our candy," Michael said. A.J. rolled her eyes before smiling.

"Yeah Mike, that was the big news this Halloween, we lost all of our candy." She shook her head. Michael stopped scrubbing her face.

"Well have you got anything else?"

"Well besides us being kidnapped and taken to a horror world literally, no."

"I still think the candy is more devastating." Michael had a stern look on his face as he looked into A.J.'s eyes.

"Oh shut up and finish scrubbing my face." Michael giggled and then she hit him in the stomach playfully. "You are so silly. I wonder why we never met before."

"School year is still young, we probably would of met eventually." He began scrubbing the makeup off again.

"Maybe you didn't notice me because I wasn't wearing any makeup or dressed up, sometimes I sneak in my mom's room and put on her makeup, it makes me look like a high school student." Michael continued to scrub the makeup off of her face. "Some guys I like think I'm not pretty without makeup."

"So you sneak back in your mom's room and steal more of her

makeup?"

"No, borrow." She had a partial smile on her face as she looked at Michael. "Mike, do you think I'm pretty without make up?" Most of her makeup was off of her face. Michael stopped scrubbing and looked directly into her face.

"I think you're very pretty without makeup."

"Thank you Michael." They starred at each other for a while.

"Guys!," a voice said.

"Ahhh!," A.J. screamed.

"OOOH!," Michael screamed.

"Sorry," Travis said. "A.J. you are needed downstairs, Theodore needs to take your picture."

"See I told you, you were pretty he wants to get a picture of you without your makeup."

"No, it's nothing like that, Michael you crazy bro. A.J. is one of the doctors, Theodore is making all of us fake id's." She took a deep breath.

"O.k. T Money, I'll be down there in a second," A.J. said. Travis left the bathroom.

"Let me get one more spot and there," Michael said as he got the last of her makeup off. He showed her the mirror.

"Wow it looks like I never had any on." A.J. smiled. She saw Michael's expression change.

"A.J. you know you don't have to go through with this whole hospital, asylum thing, I can change spots with you."

"No they need me, all of you need me."

"Especially me."

"That's very sweet." She kissed Michael. "Let's go downstairs." She grabbed his hand and they walked down the stairs. When they got downstairs they saw Benji.

"You guys look cheerful," Benji said.

"Yes I guess we do."

"Everyone except Gloria and the little boy are in the weapons room, come on." They followed Benji down to the weapons room. As soon as A.J. arrived, Theodore told her where he wanted her to stand. Once she was where he wanted her at he took her picture.

"That was the last one," Theodore said.

"So Theodore you never told us why you couldn't go," Edward said.

"Oh no, they hate my kind there."

"Remember my friends, although he may look human he is a werewolf and he was born a werewolf," Dracula said.

"I still don't understand what that means," Tim admitted.

"They can smell me and tell I'm a werewolf from a mile away," Theodore said.

"Wow, they can actually smell you?" A.J. asked in amazement.

"They are evil my friends, that is why I must warn you again to take every precaution and leave there as soon as you can," Count Dracula said. "Whatever you do don't say anything about a werewolf, they kill friends of werewolves and they will surely kill you if you mention knowing or being friends with a werewolf."

"O.k. we won't mention it," Tim said.

"It seems like these guys will kill us for anything," Michael said.

"Some doctors," Benji said.

"After you are done taking your weapons to the van you must hurry and get dressed in your doctor clothes," Dracula said. "For those of you who are not doctors we have some regular clothes in the closet upstairs."

"Great, I can't wait to get out of this," Michael said as he began taking off all of his clothes. He had his shirt off and was about to take off his pants when he realized everyone was staring at him.

"You know Michael there's rooms upstairs you can change in that won't be in front of everyone." Everyone in the room except Dracula, Theodore, Edward and A.J. laughed at him. Edward looked at him angrily while A.J. shook her head.

"He knows, come on Mike," Edward said as he pulled Michael by his ear up the stairs.

CHAPTER 8

When most of Dracula's guests got up stairs, they were surprised at all the clothes, hats, shoes, glasses, headbands and other accessories they found in his closet.

"Where did all these clothes come from?" A.J. asked.

"I don't know," Michael said.

"I still need something to wear under it." She was looking at a light red top. "That's cute, I know we can't take forever."

"You guys are complaining, I've been burning up all night in this storm trooper outfit," Tim said. He took it off and threw it to the floor.

"I gotta find something for Gloria too, wow he even has women shoes."

"This guy Drac is a playa," Travis said with a big grin on his face. "My boy Drac be getting it in."

"He's obviously rich, but it's still weird that he'd have all these clothes in all different fits."

"He likes all kind of women," Benji said.

"What about all the men and boy clothes in here?"

"That's what rich people do, spend their money on stuff they don't need."

"Still weird."

"Are you guys finding everything you need?" Dracula asked, startling some of them.

"Yeah, it's a little weird."

"Whatever are you talking about young lady?"

"You have a lot of women shoes."

"I must admit I am a ladies' man and I have lived for hundreds of years and dated thousands of women and then I met my three queens." He turned on another light and they saw a painting of Dracula with three beautiful women.

"Where are they now?"

"They died three years ago." He was quiet. "I miss them so very much, but continue, I didn't mean to bother you." He walked down the stairs. Travis waited until he was gone to speak to A.J.

"I told you he was a playa," Travis told her. A.J. rolled her eyes.

When everyone was dressed and all their weapons were loaded up they went out to the van in order to leave.

"Remember what I said, at sunset you can come back here," Dracula told them.

"So what are we supposed to do before then?" A.J. asked.

"You can come here, just make sure you are not followed, we don't want any uninvited guests." Theodore came close to Tim with a small bag in his hand.

"You may need this," Theodore said.

"What is it?" Tim asked.

"Dynamite, enough to blow up a whole room, maybe even more, don't use it unless you absolutely have to." Tim took the bag with the Dynamite in it. "Good luck.

"Yes good luck," Dracula said. Frankenstein's monster waved at them as they got into the van.

"Who's driving?" Tim asked.

"I'm driving, but we gotta find somewhere to eat," Travis said as he got in on the driver's side. He started the engine.

"Looks like we're gonna need some gas too," Michael said.

"I just thought about something," Tim said. "Do you have your license T Money?"

"No."

"Are you sure you know how to drive?"

"Yeah, I still know how to drive though, bro my Dad taught me how to drive when I was ten bro."

"Whether he does or not there shouldn't be too much traffic on the road and there will be no cops to pull him over," Gloria said. "Let's just go."

It took 20 minutes for Travis to find a gas station.

"Aye yo there's a man in there," Travis said, with surprise in his voice.

"I can't believe they have a gas station clerk," Gloria said.

"Bring a few guns just in case he isn't friendly," Tim said.

"Who's getting out?" Edward asked.

"I'll get out," A.J. said.

"You know I'm getting out," Travis said.

"I'll stay in here with the kid," Gloria said.

"I'm going, we have a long ride ahead of us," Michael said. They got out of the van and walked to the entrance of the convenient store. Benji stayed in the van with Gloria. Tim tried to open the door to get inside the convenient store but it was locked. He knocked on the door, but the clerk didn't come. He knocked again, but the clerk still didn't come. Tim became impatient and began banging on the glass door.

"Hey, hey!," he yelled. The clerk finally walked up to the door.

"What do you want?" the clerk asked.

"Food and gas."

"Yall ain't no vampires are yall?"

"Do we look like vampires to you man?" Travis asked angrily.

"I don't know what you look like, I hope you're human."

"Oh darn, we're space aliens," Travis said sarcastically.

"I knew it."

"He's kidding," Tim explained. He looked at Travis with disappointment in his face. "Remember aliens exist here and they ain't E.T."

"We're human, can we please get gas and food?" A.J. asked.

"You got money?" the clerk asked.

"Money, money, the world is a living hell and you're asking us if we have any money?" Travis asked meanly.

"I was just kidding with the last question," the old clerk said. He unlocked the door and walked away. "There's no use for too much money around here anymore," he said to them as they walked into the store. As soon as Travis got in he looked for something sweet to eat. When he saw some Twinkies he didn't wait to open it up and bite into it. "I wouldn't eat that if I were you, not until you check the expiration date." Travis looked at the wrapper he threw to the ground.

"July 89!," Travis said, with the Twinkie still in his mouth. He spit the Twinkie out on the floor.

"There is some food in here that's good. Those of us who are still alive supply it."

"Wow, how do you guys do it?" A.J. asked.

"I can't share all my secrets, but I will tell you this, there are more people alive than you think."

"What do you mean than we think?" Tim asked.

"You're not from around here are you?"

"No."

"I could tell, you look like Canadians, heard it isn't as many zombies out there, but I heard they have hell of problems with vampires."

"Yeah, we do," A.J. said.

"Yes 1993," Travis said, looking at the Twinkie wrapper. He ripped it open and began eating it.

"Well take whatever you need, I won't hold you," the clerk said walking back to his counter. "I'll turn the gas on for you." Tim looked at Edward and Travis.

"This guy could be useful to us, as far as getting information, I'm gonna see what other tips he can give us," Tim said. Tim followed the clerk back to his desk. "Aye I have a question for you."

"What is it?"

"If there are good people still alive how do I get help, or get in contact with them if we ever get in trouble?"

"I thought you guys said you were from Canada?"

"Well..."

"We visited Canada, but we are from much further than that," A.J. said as she walked beside Tim.

"Yeah, you can say it's almost like another world," Michael said as he walked to the counter with a bag full of food and drinks for everyone in the van. The gas station clerk pulled out a small black device. He pressed the on switch and an arrow flashed pointing left of the clerk. "What is that?"

"This is called the train finder, It's a highly advanced tracking device made by the government officials that made it through this depleted world," the clerk told them.

"What does it do?"

"We have a underground railroad, when you are on the streets or anywhere and you are in trouble turn on the train finder and it will point to the nearest train station. If it stays in the middle that means you are out of a train station zone."

"Well that would suck."

"But what's gonna stop the zombies from following us into the underground railroad?" Edward asked. A.J. was surprised he was there.

"Blood," the clerk said. All of them were confused.

"Blood?" many of them repeated as if it were an echo in the gas station.

"Yeah, sure, you can't get in the entrance without blood. There's a scanner, you have to put your blood up to the scanner to get in."

"So wait, we have to stab ourselves to get in?" Travis asked while he was finishing eating a Twinkie. "That's crazy."

"Stab yourself, cut yourself, scratch yourself, whatever it takes to draw blood and I suggest you do it before you get there. If you are being chased by zombies you won't have time to do it when you get there."

"But wait, won't the zombies just follow us in?" Edward asked.

"Maybe, but after one of you puts your blood to the scanner it stays open for 2 minutes." The visitors from a parallel world all looked at each other. "You have 2 minutes to get through that door before it closes and if you are in the opening it will smash you."

"Can't vampires just do the same thing, just put their blood to the scanner?" A.J. asked.

"Vampire blood is different than human blood. The door won't open for them. Also if you get infected by a zombie it won't open."

"What about werewolves?"

"Same thing, blood is different, door won't open."

"Let's say in that 2 minutes they do follow us in," Edward said.

"Who, vampires, werewolves or zombies?"

"Either one is bad."

"Well there's tons of security inside the train stations. Vampires are usually scared to step inside the train station because of all the garlic. As far as the werewolves, they are spotted by dogs inside the train station."

"That's what we haven't seen any of, we haven't seen any dogs," Michael said.

"A lot of werewolves attack them, that way they won't be identified by dogs when they're in their human form. Some dogs can even kill werewolves, depending on the dog and how good it's been trained and how strong it is. We pick up dogs off the streets and train them to make sure they don't become extinct."

"Sounds like you guys have quite the operation going on," Edward said.

"Our numbers are growing each year, we will take our world back one day, but I probably won't live to see it."

"What about your kids?" Tim asked.

"I had a family, but they were killed when all this hell on Earth first started happening."

"When did it first start happening?" Edward asked.

"And how?" Tim asked.

"Wow you guys are from another world, you've been out of it, what was the size of the rock you were sleeping under?" the clerk asked sarcastically.

"Please, we need to know."

"I really don't know how it started, I suppose I'm not the one to ask. It's been this way for about twenty years now."

"Twenty years?" Tim asked as if he hadn't heard correctly.

"Yes sir, first with serial killers that could not seem to be caught, then we had all the killings in Camp Crystal Lake, then the crime and bank robberies got worse, you'd be at the grocery store and a man would walk in with a gun and start shooting people. Then we had a virus that caused the zombies, then we had evil wizards and it just kept going on and on. Every month something more crazier than before."

"How long has the underground train station been going on?" Edward asked.

"About five years, we are all confident that it will help to clean the world up. We can transport foods, water and we have trains all over the world, I just wish my two boys could've lived to see it, cause they would be the ones to see the world change back to normal." He handed Tim the train finder. "Whatever you do don't lose this, in fact." He goes behind the counter and grabs another train finder and hands it to A.J. "Just in case you guys get separated, or lose one of them." The clerk hands them two packs of double A batteries. "It runs on double A batteries."

"Thank you for all your help," Tim said. After they got all the snacks they could carry, they walked outside. Michael opened up the van.

"I don't know what the kid likes Gloria," Michael said to her.

"What do you wanna eat honey?" Gloria asked the little boy. He pointed to the Jay's Barbeque potato chips. Gloria got it from Michael and opened it up for the little boy.

"Thank you Gloria," the little boy said.

"You welcome Robin hood."

"My name isn't Robin hood, it's Christopher."

"Well I didn't know, you told me you weren't' supposed to tell strangers your name."

"You're not a stranger no more." He began eating his potato chips.

"What am I Christopher?"

"My new friend."

"Oh that's sweet." She hugged him and smiled.

"This experience for bad or worse has brought us all together," Tim said. "As long as we have each other's back we'll be o.k. and I think everybody will have each other's back. I know deep down we're all scared, but we have a chance to go home and more importantly stop Professor Gibbs from ever doing this again." A.J. started laughing. "What's so funny A.J.?"

"The man in this world we have to save is the same man in the other world responsible for us being here," she explained.

"Yeah life throws you some unexpected twists, but if that's what we have to do to get back home, then that's what we have to do. We have to be careful with who we tell our secrets to. I don't know how many people, if any, we should tell we are from a different world and I don't think we should tell anyone about the Count and Theodore."

"I agree," Edward said.

"Do you think the Professor Gibbs of this world will know a way out of here?" Gloria asked.

"I'm sure he will, Dracula's sure he already does, we just need to get to him and find out."

"The tank is full, we can go," Travis said. He took the gas pump out of the gas tank and got into the driver's side. Everyone else got into the van. "Man I could really go for some chicken."

"Me too."

"Me three," Michael said.

"Well we're gonna have to wait and eat up on these snacks for now," Tim said as he sat in the front passenger side. "Edward you have the directions?"

"No, I think Benji has then," Edward said as he looked over at Benji.

"Don't look at me, I gave them to Michael," Benji said. Michael looked very nervous as he looked through his pockets.

"Oh my god, I don't have it,' Michael said.

"You idiot, how are we supposed to get there now?" Edward asked. People in the van started to moan and groan.

"Hold on everyone, I have the directions to the asylum," A.J. said.

"You?"

"Yeah me, I didn't trust you guys, sorry Mike, but I thought you would lose it."

"We probably would have," Michael admitted. Edward smacked Michael. "Oh."

"Good thinking A.J.," Tim said, as he held out his hand. She gave him the directions.

Half way through the drive Travis got tired and let Tim drive the rest of the way. When they got to the asylum it was still early. Edward, Benji and Tim were the only ones who were awake in the van. Tim didn't want to park directly in front of the asylum until 6am, the time the building opened to non-workers.

"We'll park here for now," Tim said. "If you guys wanna get some rest and I be the first look out you can, I'm glad Theodore gave all of us watches."

"I slept for a long time, I'm wide awake," Edward said.

"Well you do first look out, I'm bushed."

"I'm assuming that means tired," Benji said.

"You bet it means I'm tired, wake me up at 5:30, I don't wanna go into the asylum drowsy."

"We'll stay up and guard the van."

"Remember if either one of you starts getting tired wake one of them up and they can watch over the van." Benji and Edward nod their heads. "Alright fellas goodnight."

"Goodnight," they tell Tim. "That's about a hour," Edward told Benji. "How are you?"

"I'll make it, but at 5 I wanna rest, will you be o.k. or will I have to wake someone else to stay up with you?" Benji asked.

"I'll be fine, I don't wanna wake up Michael, he has to stay in here when we go inside, he needs all of his rest."

CHAPTER 9

When it was time to go inside the asylum all the people in the van who were going were nervous. Tim made sure they all knew what to say and what not to say and what to do and what not to do. He also made sure they were all wearing their identification cards. Edward drove up to the asylum and parked the van. He got out as Travis got out on the passenger side. Travis opened the sliding van door for the others who were getting out. After they were out Tim looked at Michael and Gloria.

"Can either one of you drive?" Tim asked.

"I can, but Edward always complains I drive too fast," Michael said.

"Well that's a good thing, just in case we have to make a run. Well in about 15 minutes get in the driver's side. Remember if you are seen out here to say you are family of Doctor O'Connor and Doctor Whittaker, say you are having family day at the job."

"Right."

"Tim," Gloria said.

"What?"

"Good luck."

"Thanks." Tim shut the sliding door of the van. They walked to the front entrance of the asylum. They opened the door and walked to the counter. They saw a woman wearing a surgical mask at the counter.

"Yes, how may I help you?" she asked.

"Yes I'm Doctor O'Connor and these are my colleges. We are here from Amityville Research, Count Dracula sent us."

"Let me see your paper work." Tim had a small suitcase in his hand. He got out the paperwork Theodore made for him and gave it to the woman. "And what is the nature of your visit?"

"We are here to study the patient you call Gibbs, we actually would like to transfer him to the Dungeon Hall Asylum."

"O.k. hold on I will call for the lead doctor." She picked up the phone. "Doctor Miller, there are some doctors from Amityville Research here to see you about Arthur Gibbs and a possible transfer, o.k., o.k." She hung up the phone. "You can take a seat, Doctor Miller will be here to see you in a few minutes." She handed Tim his paper work back. They sat down on both sides of the check-in desk. They were all afraid to say anything for fear of looking suspicious. They instead looked down at the floor, fidgeted with their hands and looked up at the wall. It wasn't long before Doctor Miller arrived. He was a tall man that looked to be Caucasian with brown eyes. He also was wearing a surgical mask.

"Hello, I'm Doctor Miller," he said as Tim stood up in order to shake his hand.

"Hi, I'm Doctor O'Connor, this is Doctor Whittaker, Doctor Dice, Doctor Robinson and Doctor Torres," Tim said. Doctor Miller shook all of their hands.

"Welcome to Homicidal Asylum. First I will show you a tour of our facilities then I will take you to Gibbs, will that be o.k.?"

"Yes." They followed Doctor Miller.

"There isn't much on the first floor so I will take you to the 6th floor first." He pressed the elevator button. When the elevator door opened they saw another doctor with a surgical mask over his face walk out. "After you." They got on the elevator followed by Doctor Miller. When he got in he pressed the button for the sixth floor. Tim and his friends were very nervous once the doors shut and the elevator began moving, they didn't know what to expect. The doors of the elevator opened. "Here we are." They all got out of the elevator. "Hopefully you won't be alarmed, I know you work with The Count, but we hate vampires and we do several experiments on them."

"If you hate vampires so much why do you work with The Count?" Benji asked.

"He has more sense than most of his kind, follow me." They looked into a glass room. They saw a dead man lying on a table with blood dripping from his neck. In front of him there was a window. The light from the window was shining on him. On the opposite side of the room in the dark there was a vampire. He was breathing hard and making weird screeching sounds. "You'll find this experiment interesting Doctor O'Connor, will a vampire come into the light to eat even though he knows it will kill him?" Tim looked at Doctor Miller, but did not respond. "If he doesn't have blood it will kill him, if he goes in to the light it will kill him, what will he do?"

"How long has he been there?"

"Two days, we remove the man at night."

"Won't the man turn into a vampire?" Edward asked.

"No, although we made it look like he was bitten he wasn't."

"How was he killed?" A.J. asked.

"We killed this man."

"Why?" Benji asked.

"For this experiment of course, you know science means having to murder a few to find out the truth sometimes, it's all about sacrifice."

"Even if it means taking a innocent man's life?" A.J. asked.

"Well Doctor Robinson no one is innocent, we all sin, we should all burn in hell, this man was killed so we could all learn the truth, it was the only way."

"Absolutely," Travis said.

"Right," Edward said. The screeching sound the vampire made gave A.J. goosebumps.

"Moving on," Doctor Miller said. A.J. was relieved they were walking away. "In this room we have a human man tied to this table. We want to see how much he can be stabbed until he swears all allegiance to the prince of darkness instead of Jesus Christ of Nazareth. So far he's been stabbed five times already and he's still saying God is his savior." When some of the visitors from another world looked in the room, they became frightened when they saw a black man in his early thirties in obvious pain. Although he was tied to the table, he was not laying down. The ropes had him tied from his waist to the back of the table. The table was tall enough to where the man's legs could dangle in the air. There was a chair on the table that the doctors had wrapped his hands around with another rope. The three doctors in the room were all wearing surgical masks.

"So who is your savior?" one of the doctors asked him.

"Jesus Christ," the man responded. The doctor stabbed the man twice, once in his shoulder and then he was stabbed in his side. "Ahhhhhhhhh!" A.J. couldn't believe this room was worse than the first one. Her first reaction was to save him. She ran towards the glass, but was immediately held back by Benji. While the man was screaming Tim looked away. The screaming sent chills down Edward's spine and it made Travis' stomach hurt. Benji had to pretend he didn't see what he saw in order to keep the facade of being a doctor.

"What about now, who do you say your prayers to?" the same doctor asked the man.

"I pray to Jesus Christ, my lord and savior," the tied up man said in between deep breaths.

"Wrong answer!" The doctor shoved two knives into his knees and did not pull either one out.

"Ahhhhhhhh! Have mercy!"

"Look, look, look," Tim told himself. He knew Doctor Miller would be suspicious of him if he didn't watch the man being tortured. He forced himself to look at the man scream as blood fell from his body unto the floor.

"Our father, which art in heaven, hallowed be thy name. Thy kingdom come. Thy will be done on Earth, as it is in heaven. Give us this day our daily bread. And forgive us our trespasses, As we forgive those who trespass against us."

"I'll put him out of his misery," Doctor Miller said. He pulled out a gun and shot through the glass.

"And deliver us from evil." The bullet connected with the man's forehead, he died instantly. A.J. had tears in her eyes, Edward felt like crying, while Benji had a mind-boggling expression on his face. Tim couldn't believe it.

"Maybe next time I'll have more patience and see how long it takes for him to bleed out or submit to Lucifer, I just hate that prayer."

"Me too, it's so drag," A.J. said. The others were happy with what she said, they were expecting her to break down, instead she continued to play the part. They walked away from the window. One of the windows they walked by they saw zombies in. They began beating against the glass when they passed.

"Never mind the zombies, that glass is perfectly safe." When they got to the next room they saw a vampire on a table wearing something over his head and on his mouth. "If you liked that Doctor Robinson you'll definitely like this." Doctor Miller looked at A.J. "We are using shock treatment on vampires to see if that can stop their craving for human blood." They saw that the doctor in the room was wearing a surgical mask. Once he flipped the switch on the machine in the room the vampires head hit the table in front of him continuously.

"How is it working so far?" Travis asked.

"So far we haven't made as much progress as I would've liked to make. Whenever we bring a human in there this vampire seems to attack him quicker, almost as if this process is speeding up the vampires need to feed." They walked away from the room. "Next we go downstairs to the weapons division." They walked back to the elevator. The visitors were happy to leave that floor, but they were all ready to leave the asylum. Once they were on the elevator they went to the fourth floor and got off. They were surprised to see more weapons on the fourth floor than they did at Count Dracula's castle. The whole floor were rooms filled with weapons of all kind. "The weapons division is used for our experiments as well for our safety, for instance these are silver bullets, the one thing that can kill a werewolf and we hate werewolves here. We also have a lot of silver for vampires and garlic sprays." A.J. smiled.

"I bet you vampires really hate that garlic spray," A.J. said.

"Oh they hate it, spray it in their mouth and they become defenseless. I saw one choke to death after being sprayed in the mouth."

"Garlic affects them that much?" Tim asked.

"Yes it does."

"Sorry, I haven't had that much experience with vampires, I like studying zombies myself."

"Yes, they are very interesting creatures to study." Doctor

Miller walked out of the room that the garlic sprays and silver bullets were in. A.J. see's Tim Grab some silver bullets and five garlic sprays. He winked at A.J. and handed her one of the garlic sprays.

"Just in case," Tim told her.

The last floor Doctor Miller showed them was the 5th floor.

"This floor is where we keep our most extreme patients, the one we call Gibbs is on this floor," Doctor Miller said. All of the patients were in cells on the floor. A.J. was startled when she saw Brenda in one of the cells. She pointed it out to Benji.

"Brenda's a zombie now," Benji said, quietly to A.J. Brenda was grabbing on the bars and screaming.

"Unless you wanna become a zombie I wouldn't get too close to her." A.J. moved away. As they continued to walk pass the cells A.J. heard someone trying to get her attention.

"Aye, aye, aye," she heard. When she turned around she was startled to see a familiar face.

"Benji come here," A.J. said.

"It's o.k. Doctor Dice, if you see any interesting patients you wanna take a closer look at be my guest, just be careful, some of them are extremely dangerous," Doctor Miller said. Benji walked over to A.J., who was still in front of the cell.

"Benji look who it is," A.J. said.

"It's Superman," Benji said. It was the 8th grader Mark, he was still wearing his Superman costume, minus the cape.

"Where's your girlfriend, the one dressed as Lois Lane?"

"They just took her, something about a experiment room," Mark said.

"Shoot!"

"What's wrong?"

"We gotta get her out of here."

"What's wrong, what kind of experiments will they do to her?"

"We don't know, and that's what scares us," Benji said.

"They could just kill her," A.J. said.

"Why, why would they do that?" Mark asked.

"These people are evil Superman, pure evil, they don't care

about anyone, they have no compassion." A.J. explained.

"Why, they're just like us." A.J. shook her head.

"They might look like us, but I don't think they're human."

"We can debate on that later," Benji said. "We gotta get to Lois."

"Monica," Mark said.

"Dang we gotta save Monica too?"

"No my girl, that's her real name, Monica."

"And what's yours?" A.J. asked.

"Mark."

"Alright we're gonna have to get you outta here too, but don't leave the cell till we tell you."

"I can't leave the cell even if I wanted too."

"I'll tell Travis to pick the lock."

"I'll go upstairs with you, hold on A.J.," Benji said. Benji told Travis about Mark and Monica and he agreed to pick the lock. Benji ran back to A.J. and they walked to the elevator. Once they pressed the button they waited nervously for it to get to their floor. When the doors opened no one got out.

"Good, those doctors are creepy." They walked in the elevator and pressed the button for floor six. Once the door shut A.J. looked over at Benji. "You have any weapons on you Benji?"

"Naw, I forgot to grab one, how about you?"

"I have this." A.J. pulled out a gun from her purse. "Theodore said it's a silencer too."

"Perfect, but hopefully we don't have to use it." When the doors of the elevator opened both Benji and A.J. felt nervous, almost scared. "What if we get stopped, what are we gonna tell them?"

"We'll just tell them Doctor Miller said we could walk around and we could observe certain experiments that we find interesting."

"And what's the plan for getting Monica out?"

"That I don't know."

CHAPTER 10

While Edward and Tim were with Doctor Miller, Travis was picking the lock on Mark's cell. Someone came behind him.

"Hey what are you doing?" the doctor in the surgical mask asked him.

"This lock looks funny to me, can you see what it says on the lock?" Travis asked him. Travis moved out of the way and then let the doctor get closer. As soon as he bent down Travis grabbed his head and pounded it against the lock which caused the doctor to lose consciousness.

"Hurry," Mark told Travis. He finished picking the lock and then grabbed the doctor and put him in the cell.

"Switch clothes with him, hurry."

"I can't get this mask off."

"Don't worry about that, I saw where there were some extra ones, wait here, I'll be right back. He should be out a while." Travis went to the elevator.

Meanwhile Doctor Miller, Edward and Tim were at Professor Gibbs' cell.

"This is the one you are looking for, Arthur Gibbs," Doctor Miller said. Edward and Tim were surprised to see how different he looked. "He hasn't said a single word in ten days. I don't know how much fun you'll have studying him if he's not gonna talk. He used to have a great imagination and talk about another world he had been to before, now he's quiet, but I will give you authorization for the transfer, just give me a few minutes." Doctor Miller walked away. Tim turned around and was surprised he and Edward were the only ones there.

"I don't like this Edward, we need to stay together," Tim said.

"I know, but they saw the guy from earlier who was dressed like Superman and Clark Kent. I guess his girlfriend is here too," Edward told Tim.

"I guess I can't get mad at going to save somebody."

"Save, I haven't heard that word in a long time," Professor Gibbs said. They were shocked he could still speak. "I'm used to hearing kill, destroy, murder, evil, not save."

"Professor Gibbs you can talk?"

"Of course I can talk, I just stopped doing it for them."

"Professor Gibbs," Edward said.

"Wait, wait, wait, I'm not worthy of that name anymore, just call me Gibbs, now go on with what you were saying."

"We came to get you out, we need you to help us."

"Me, help you, how could I?"

"By getting us home, back to our reality, back to our dimension," Tim said. Gibbs turned his back on Edward and Tim.

"I don't know what you are talking about."

"Please Gibbs, we know you're not crazy, we just wanna go home!"

"Shhhh Tim, someone may hear you," Edward said.

"They might as well hear me cause if we don't get him to help us we will die here, I don't wanna die here, I wanna go home." Gibbs turned around to face them again.

"You're not a devil worshipper, serial killer, alien that looks human?" Gibbs asked them.

"No, we're one hundred percent human."

"Well in that case I think I can help you."

"Yes," Tim said as he gave Edward a high five.

Meanwhile A.J. and Benji were on the 6th floor.

"Which way should we go?" Benji asked A.J.

"I don't know, she could be anywhere," A.J. said. "We have to look everywhere until we find her." They walked straight after exiting the elevator. They were surprised none of the doctors or nurses looked at them. "Benji you see how many of them there are?" she asked him in a soft voice.

"Yeah."

"If we have to run back to the elevator how are we gonna make it without being stopped?"

"Why you asking me, you are the one coming up with all the

plans."

Travis made it back to Mark.

"I got the mask bro," Travis said. "I got this too." Travis had a small container with a needle. He put the needle in the container and then poked the needle into the unconscious doctor's neck. "Sweet dreams." Mark, who already had on the doctors clothes put on the surgical mask and walked out of the cell. "That's strong stuff, according to the bottle they use that on patients here and sometimes they are out for a whole day."

"I'm ready to get Monica,"' Mark said.

"I'm sorry, but I can't let you bro."

"What?"

"Don't worry we got two people up there who would give their life for her if it came to that, but I'm confident they will find her and bring her back alive."

"Well what do you want me to do, just wait on the sidelines?"

"No, actually wait in the van."

"Van, how'd you guys get a van out here?"

"It's a long story bro, I'll have to tell you about it later. Right now we gotta go." They shut the cell. When they turned around a doctor wearing a surgical mask was right behind them.

"What is he doing in there?" the doctor asked.

"Nothing," Travis answered.

"Yeah, he's dead asleep," Mark, who now looked like one of the doctors that worked there said.

"Good, he's so ugly to look at," the doctor said. He walked away from them.

"Let's go," Travis said. When they got to the entrance the woman at the counter asked them a question.

"You coming back Hun?" she asked.

"Yeah, it's family day and some of my family wants to talk to this doctor."

"O.k. come back soon."

"Sure." Travis smiled at the lady. They walked out of the Homicidal Asylum.

On the 6th floor A.J. and Benji looked for Monica. They looked in one room and saw a vampire being sliced in his face with a butcher knife. They also saw bugs being forced in a human woman's mouth.

"We better make sure we don't get caught, I'm afraid to find out what they would do to us," Benji said.

"We'll get out Benji," A.J. said. They heard a female voice screaming. They ran to the sound and saw that it was Monica. She was being forced into one of the rooms by two doctors wearing surgical masks.

"But I wanna see!," Monica pleaded with them.

"But we want to test your senses, without your eyes you'll be forced to use your sense of smell, your sense of taste and your ears," one of the doctors told her.

"No, no, no!"

"We gotta stop this," A.J. said. They ran after her, but the door shut before they could get inside the room. They could see the doctors and Monica through the window. Benji began banging on the window.

"Go see what he wants," one of the doctors told the other. The Doctor opened the door.

"Yes what is it?" she asked.

"We would like to come in, we're from Amityville Research," A.J. told the doctor.

"I'm sorry we can have no visitors in here with us, if you're interested in watching just view from the glass."

"Can I ask you one more thing?" The doctor rolled her eyes.

"Yes, what is it?"

"Have you ever seen this before?" She pulled out her gun and shot the doctor which caused her to fall to the floor. The other doctor tried to get to the alarm, but A.J. shot him and he fell to the floor. Monica was relieved to see them.

"I recognize you guys, you go to my school," Monica said.

"Yes we do, we gotta go," Benji said. Monica screamed. When Benji turned around he saw the first doctor A.J. shot was on her feet. When she took off her mask Benji was surprised not to see any lips. She pulled both sides of her face where a human's mouth would be. She pulled it back until Benji could see a mouth with teeth. Unlike humans her mouth was narrow and her teeth were only on the side of her mouth and not across. She let out an eerie scream that was very loud. When her tongue, which was much longer and bigger in size than a humans tongue came out of her mouth it grabbed Benji by his legs. "Help, help, help!" A.J. shot at the creature, but it continued to hold on to Benji. She swung Benji around with her tongue. Monica screamed again which caused A.J. to turn her attention away from Benji. The other doctor was now standing on his feet. A.J. punched him before he could take off his mask. A.J. was surprised he did not fall. He smacked A.J. off her feet which caused her to drop the gun. He took off his mask and let out a similar scream. Monica grabbed the gun as the doctor's tongue came at A.J. She shot at the doctor's tongue, missing the first three times. On the fourth attempt Monica connected with the doctor's tongue. The doctor let out a scream and then grabbed Monica's leg with his tongue and dragged her towards him. He tried to take a bite out of her, but Monica shot him in the mouth. The back of his head had a hole in it which caused him to fall over dead. The other creature let out a scream when she saw her colleague was dead. She dropped Benji on the floor and made her way quickly towards Monica. She grabbed her with her hands and picked Monica up by her neck. She let out a scream.

"Throw it!," A.J. said. Monica with the rest of her strength, threw the gun to A.J. Once A.J. had the gun she shot the creature in its back. She let out a scream and then dropped Monica. Benji got to his feet, but avoided the doctor. The doctor tried to grab A.J. with her tongue.

"Duck!," Monica said. A.J. fell to the ground, barley missing the doctor's tongue. The doctor lost her balance due to Benji and Monica pushing her from behind with a rolling chair. She was rolled into the machine they were going to use to poke out Monica's eyes, instead the needles went through the doctor's mouth, killing her instantly. They all stared at the dead doctors.

"O.k. leader what should we do now?" Benji asked A.J.

"Funny Benji," A.J. said. "At this point let's get the heck out of here and stay alive doing it." They slowly walked out of the room.

"How are you on ammunition?"

"I'm still good."

"I wish I had a gun."

"I wish we were home," Monica said.

"Yeah, we all wish that," Benji said. They saw some doctors in front of them that were all wearing surgical masks.

"O.k. whatever you guys do don't look suspicious," A.J. warned them. "Don't even make a lot of eye contact with the doctors."

"Is it o.k. if I walk with my head down?" Monica asked.

"Yeah it's o.k."

"What are those things?" Benji asked.

"I don't know, but I told you they weren't human."

"How did you know?"

"Certain things Doctor Miller was saying."

"How do they talk under those masks?"

"I don't know, some form of hypnosis or they have a different way of communicating, now shhh." The doctors on the floor began to stare at them as they made their way to the elevator.

"Um, A.J. I think they are staring at us," Benji said.

"I thought I told you not to look."

"Well I took a glance and I saw all eyes on us."

"We're almost to the elevator." One of the doctors walked in front of them.

"Excuse me," she said. Benji rolled his eyes while Monica and A.J. tried to remain calm.

"Yes maam?"

"Where do you think you are going with her, she's supposed to have her eyes taken out today."

"The doctors found a better specimen."

"Why wasn't I notified, I'm one of the lead doctors on this floor."

"Doctor Miller just called us," Benji said.

"Oh o.k., let me clarify it with him, stay here." She walked to one of the hospital phones. As soon as her back was turned A.J., Monica, and Benji ran to the elevator. "Hey wait."

"I hope that elevator is ready."

"No time, stairs, we still have to get the others," A.J. said.

They ran down the stairs as they heard the doctor continue to tell them to wait. The doctor pressed the alarm.

Doctor Miller walked back to Edward and Tim with the paperwork.

"Here you are, the transfer has been approved, I just need you to sign it Doctor O'Connor," Doctor Miller said as he gave Tim the paperwork.

"Can you let him out?" Tim asked.

"Oh yes, how forgetful of me." Doctor Miller unlocked the door. "He usually doesn't try to run so he should be good." Tim was feeling out the paperwork when he heard the alarm. "That's strange, why is the alarm going off?" Edward and Tim looked at each other. They heard the phone ring. "Hold on doctors, I'll be right back." He walked to the nearest phone.

"I think that's our cue to go," Edward said to Tim.

"I think you're right," Tim said. They snuck away to the elevator with Gibbs. Edward pressed the down button and the elevator signaled that it was coming to their floor. When it opened they saw one of the doctors in their true form.

"Naaaw!" It got out of the elevator and began choking Edward.

"Get off him!" It elbowed Tim in his head which caused him to fall down on his back. When he looked up he saw another one of the creatures looking down at him. It let out a scream and then proceeded to stomp Tim's head. Tim rolled over to avoid being seriously injured. One of the creatures grabbed Gibbs.

"I guess you're going back," the creature said to him without moving its mouth.

"That's what you think!," A.J. said as the doorway leading to the stairs closed. When she shot the creature it went through its mouth. It screamed before falling to the ground. A.J. shot the creature choking Edward which caused it to let him go, but it was still alive. It tried to attack Edward again. He grabbed his knife and sliced the creature in its neck. Edward saw green blood from the creature's neck. Soon the blood disappeared and the creature was healed.

"What the.....," Edward said. The creature screamed.

"Put the knife in his mouth Edward!" Edward threw it in its mouth. The creature put both of its hands on its neck and then fell on the floor. "Doctor Miller!" Doctor Miller, who's mask was also off as he tried to kill them turned and looked at A.J. "Didn't know which one you were, for the record I am a Christian and Jesus Christ is my savior." He jumped towards her as she fired her gun at him. When her bullets connected with his mouth, Doctor Miller was dead. Monica ran to the elevator door as it was shutting.

"Hurry, I can't hold it," Monica said.

"Get in!," Tim said as he punched one of the creatures, knocking him to the ground.

"What about T Money?" A.J. asked, as she shot at the creatures.

"He's already outside with Mark." All of them ran to the elevator as the creatures attacked them from every direction. The creature Tim knocked to the floor grabbed his leg with his tongue which caused Tim to fall down.

"Come on Tim!" Tim grabbed his knife and cut the creatures tongue in half. He got up and ran to the elevator. As he was running, he threw his knife at one of the creatures, striking it in the forehead, thus the creature fell to the ground. Edward continued to shoot the creatures as they rushed the elevator.

"O.k. shut the door!," Edward yelled. As the elevator doors were closing they saw one of the creatures run to the doors. Once the doors shut the creature reopened them. A.J. shot it in its mouth and the doors shut again.

"Wow A.J. where'd you learn to shoot like that?" Tim asked.

"This is my first day ever using a gun," she told him. Tim was very surprised and they could all see it in his expression.

"I guess you're a natural then, lucky for us." As the elevator went down they were all breathing hard. When the elevator signaled they were on the first floor they all looked at each other. "O.k. very quiet you guys." The doors stayed shut. They almost didn't want them to open. When they opened they looked out in front of them and did not see anyone.

"Something's not right."

"Yeah, you would think they would be waiting for us,"

Edward said.

"Shh, it may be a trap," Tim said. "Edward you got your gun ready?"

"Yep."

" A.J. you have enough bullets?"

"Enough to get out of here," A.J. said.

"Benji you don't have any weapon?"

"I left mine in the van," Benji said.

"Dang Benji."

"Yeah, dang Benji," Edward said. Edward hit him in his forehead with his gun.

"Monica you stay close to me, Gibbs stay close to Edward."

"Sure," Gibbs said.

"But Tim, where's your gun?" A.J. asked.

"I don't have any more ammo, I have these two guns," Tim said as he balled his fists. A.J. smiled. "Let's go." They slowly walked out of the elevator. They looked around, but didn't see any of the creatures. Tim looked above his head and saw twenty or more of the creatures on the ceiling. All of them began screaming. A.J., Benji, Gibbs, Edward and Monica saw that they were on the ceiling. One of the creatures grabbed Monica with its hands and lifted her off her feet while it stayed on the ceiling. Monica screamed as A.J. tried to shoot the creature. It knocked the gun out of her hand. Edward got a knife out of his pocket and sliced the creature's hands that were holding Monica. The creature screamed as Monica fell to the floor. Edward began shooting the creatures on the ceiling. After five shots the creatures jumped off the ceiling and surrounded them. "Uhh guys I hate to say this, but I can't help but notice we're a little outnumbered," Tim said.

"A little?" Edward asked meanly.

"They'll probably kill all of us," Gibbs said. The van they drove to the asylum crashed in through one of the side windows. The impact made many of the creatures lose their balance and fall.

"That looks like our ride," Tim said

"We still can't get to it, it's to many of them," Benji said. Travis opened the passenger door and got out holding two guns. He began firing them at every creature he saw.

"Yeah, yeah, yeah!," Travis said as he shot the creatures. "This is easier than I thought!" One of the creatures grabbed Travis' leg with its tongue. He fell down, dropping his guns.

"idiot!," A.J. said. The creature banged Travis against the ceiling and the walls with its tongue. Mark got out of the van and shot the creature in its mouth. The creature and Travis fell to the floor. Travis looked spooked as he moved the tongue off of his leg. He looked up at Mark.

"Thanks."

"You welcome," Mark said. Two more creatures jumped in front of Mark and Travis. The horn of the van was heard. Travis and Mark moved out of the way. The van went in reverse, smashing many of the creatures. The back door of the van opened. A.J., Benji, Edward, Tim, Monica and Gibbs saw Gloria.

"Get in," she said. They began to get into the van. One of the creatures tried to pull Tim's arm with his hand. Tim punched it in its face, consequentially the creature fell to the ground. Travis regained his guns and shot at the creature before getting in the passenger side. Mark tried to get in on the sliding door, but was pulled by a tongue of one of the creatures on the ceiling.

"Mark!," Monica screamed.

"Get his hand!," Tim yelled. Edward pulled his hand.

"I'm losing my grip, help me pull him!," Edward said. A.J. got behind him and pulled Mark's hand. Tim got close by the door and started shooting at the creature. After three shots the creature fell from the ceiling and let go of Mark. They were able to pull Mark into the van. They shut the sliding door. They heard the creatures jumping on the top of the van. Some of the creatures were on the back of the van pushing it.

"They're gonna try to tip us!," Gloria said.

"They're not doing that bad of a job right now!"

"Mike, get us outta here," Tim said.

"Thought you never ask," Michael said. He stepped on the gas pedal, moving the van in reverse, running over five of the creatures. He turned around the van as he smashed into one of their desks.

"What are you doing Mike?" Travis asked.

"We're going out the front."

"Why not the way we came?"

"It'll be harder to lose them in the woods, we know the front leads to the main road."

"What if we tip?" Everyone in the van became quiet, except for Christopher, he was crying in Gloria's arms.

"That's a chance we'll have to take," Tim said. "Everyone brace yourselves." As they drove towards the front entrance a creature stood up in front of the van. It let out a scream before being ran over by the van.

"Sorry but you didn't have the crosswalk," Michael said, which caused people in the van to laugh. The van shattered the windows on the entrance doors. The van wobbled as they went down the stairs.

"Please don't tip, please don't tip," A.J. prayed in her head. Monica and Mark hugged each other as the van wobbled.

"We're gonna tip, we're gonna tip!," Benji yelled. Tim shook his head.

"Shut up!," Edward said. He hit Benji in his head with his gun. They were coming to the end of the stairs. "You should be able to jump the rest of those stairs, floor it!" Michael stepped hard on the gas pedal. The van lifted high into the air as the people inside screamed. When the van hit the ground they were all relieved. The van stopped moving.

"Wow cool Mike, can we do it again?" Christopher asked.

"No I don't think so little man," Michael said.

"Now get us outta here," Edward said.

"Right away." Michael tried to go, but the van wouldn't move. He put the van back in park and tried to start it again. "It's not letting me start it again." He turned the key counter clock wise and then turned the key clock wise, but the van did not start.

"What's wrong?"

"I don't know, it's not starting." Michael tried starting the van again, but it didn't start. Each time he would try to start it and it didn't start people in the van became more anxious and nervous.

They heard the screams the creatures make.

"Uhh Mike get this thing going!," Edward said nervously. He saw the creatures running down the stairs.

"I'm trying, I'm trying, come on!" He turned the key and the engine turned on.

"Go!," Tim said loudly. Michael stepped on the gas pedal so hard the people in the van thought he was going to crash, he nearly tipped over on the turn.

CHAPTER 11

"Wow what an escape," A.J. said.

"I thought we were some goners," Edward said.

"Me too," Benji said.

"Thanks for getting us out of there," Monica said. Mark nodded his head.

"Well we couldn't leave you there," Tim said.

"Some people would," Mark said.

"Not me, as soon as A.J. told me you were here I knew it was the right thing to do, I knew it would make it harder, but I knew it was the right thing to do."

"How did you guys know we were in trouble?" Monica asked Mark.

"Me, Michael and T Money heard the alarms going off, we woke Gloria and Christopher up and told them we had to go in after you," Mark explained.

"From what I saw being in there for only a short time, patients don't escape out of there."

"No, they never do," Gibbs said.

"We figured if the alarm is sounding you guys must be in trouble," Travis said.

"If you wouldn't have got there we would of died," A.J. said.

"I wasn't gonna let that happen A.J.," Michael said.

"Thank you Michael." She smiled at Michael and he saw it when he looked at her in the rearview mirror.

"So what's the plan?" Mark asked.

"Well we have Professor Gibbs, he should be able to get us home," Michael said.

"Please Gibbs, and yes, I should be able to get you home," he said. Everyone in the van cheered. "However I cannot seem to remember how to operate the machine, I do recall I left some notes for myself at my old place."

"Great, where is it?" Tim asked.

"Los Angeles."

"According to the map that's a long way from here."

"And we're gonna have to stop for gas soon," Michael said.

"Something I wanna know guys," Gibbs said.

"What is it?" Tim asked.

"How did you know who I am and where I was?"

"Well we come from a parallel dimension," Edward explained.

"Yes, I got that part, go on."

"The you or Professor Gibbs from our world is evil, he sent us here to teach us a lesson."

"Teach you a lesson, I don't understand, what do you mean?"

"He never went trick or treating as a kid, he wanted to show us what true horror was," Tim said.

"And he sure did," Gloria said.

"Although the Professor Gibbs of your world is, in a sense me, he is nothing like me. I lived my life right and when I was a child I did go trick or treating," Gibbs said. The people in the van looked surprised.

"You even look different than him."

"Oh?"

"Yeah, he looks more, more, mad, evil or insane," A.J. explained to him.

"He must be, why would he send kids to a place like this, how many of you guys were there, just you in the van?" Everyone in the van became very quiet.

"Professor, it was at least 50 or more of us in those cages," Gloria said.

"50, it was at least 100," Tim said.

"I don't think it was 100," Benji said.

"Guys the point is it was a large number of us in those cages," Gloria said.

"Cages?" Gibbs asked.

"Yeah Professor Gibbs, he put us in cages and then transported all of us from the cages here," Tim said. Gibbs had a saddened look on his face.

"We don't know how many of us from our world are still alive," Benji said.

"That's awful, but o.k., how'd you know I was here?" Gibbs asked.

"Count Dracula told us," Edward said.

"Count Dracula?" Mark asked. "I thought he was a bad guy."

"No, on this world he's actually a good guy. He's the one that gave us all the weapons and this van."

"Oh." Mark began laughing.

"Dracula, Dracula," Gibbs said.

"What's wrong Professor?" Tim asked.

"Dracula."

"Dracula is your friend, remember Dracula is your friend," Gibbs heard in his head.

"Dracula is my friend," Gibbs mumbled.

"What did you say?" Benji asked.

"I said Dracula is my friend."

"Oh he is?"

"Yeah, I actually remember.....hmm, I can't seem to remember too much about the fella, except he visited me and tried to get me out, but those Camadeians wouldn't let me go."

"Camadeians?" Tim asked.

"Yeah, the doctors, those things that were trying to stop us from escaping, they are called Camadeians."

"I always wanted to be a comedian," Benji said, trying to joke around. Edward hit him in his head with his fist.

"Say Gibbs, where do those things come from?" Edward asked.

"No one knows exactly, but somewhere in outer space, far from our galaxy," Gibbs said. They felt a bump and Michael nearly lost control of the van.

"What kind of driving are you doing Mike?"

"That's not me, something's wrong," Michael said. The van came to a complete stop. "Let me get out to see what's wrong."

"I'll get out with you," Travis said as he grabbed a shot gun. They got out of the van and noticed the two front tires were flat.

"How did that happen?"

"Looks like you just had a blowout."

"I don't think so." Michael found a stick with spikes on it and little skulls with spikes under the van. "Someone did this on purpose." He knocked on the window of the van. Edward rolled down the window. "We gotta get outta here and fast."

"That bad?" Tim asked.

"I'm not sure, maybe worse." Michael showed him what he found. Gibbs was curious, so he looked at what Michael had in his hand.

"Cannibals," Gibbs said.

"You mean cannibals like the ones who eat people?"

"Yeah, they are here."

"Alright everyone get as many weapons as you can carry, we have to go," Tim said. An arrow hit the van. Michael and Travis looked into the woods and they could see twenty cannibals in the distance. None of them looked human, they all had physical deformities on their faces that caused them to look more like animals than human. To the visitors on the parallel world, they looked like monsters. They began running towards the van. Tim who saw them from the window was worried some of them would be killed in a matter of seconds. "Get out!"

"Alright Chris get on my back again," Gloria told Christopher as she bent down. He got on her back as Travis reloaded his shot gun. When A.J. got the train finder out of her pocket she pressed the on switch in order to see where the nearest train station was.

"You guys are not gonna believe this," A.J. said.

"I almost don't wanna know," Benji said.

"What is it?" Tim asked as they hid behind the van.

"We can't run this way," A.J. said, pointing in front of her. She turned the opposite direction. "The train finder is pointing that way." She pointed to the woods, where the cannibals were coming from.

"Great!" Tim shot at the cannibals, using the van as a shield. "T Money, we gotta take out the ones with bow and arrows."

"I'm with you," Travis said. There were three cannibals with bow and arrows. Travis shot two of them. Tim looked at him with a serious expression and then smiled.

"That's what I call service." The last cannibal with a bow and arrow ran into the woods. The other cannibals were so upset that two of them were killed that they threw their weapons into the air. One of the weapons they threw was a spike bat. Gloria crotched low by the van, covering Christopher's head as the weapons came down. Mark, Monica, Michael, Benji, Tim and A.J. ran away from the van. Travis snuck in the van and lit the explosives with the lighter Theodore gave him. He grabbed Gloria and Christopher as the cannibals got closer to the van.

"Run you guys!" The cannibals made their way to the van.

"Everybody down!," Tim said, right before the van exploded. All of the cannibals were destroyed. Tim got off the ground slowly. "Is everyone o.k.?" He looked around and was relieved everyone was alright. "Everyone has to get up and run like hell through those woods to the train station." Some of them were moving slow. "I know all of us are tired, but we have to go, there may be more of those things." Tim got in front of everyone. "I'll lead, T Money you cover the back."

"Yes sir."

"Anyone that has weapons get them out." They followed Tim as he ran on the trail in the woods. Travis held his shot gun to the trees as he ran. Gibbs was directly in front of him, while A.J. was behind Tim. The leaves on one of the trees moved, causing everyone to freeze. Tim saw a raccoon in the tree. "It's just a raccoon, come on."

"How much further?" A.J. asked Tim, who was using his train finder.

"I don't know, it's still pointing straight ahead."

"Are you sure you're reading that thing right?"

"Yeah, come on we need to be quiet." They continued to walk until the train finder pointed to the left. "Dang."

"What's wrong Tim?" Benji asked as everyone on the trail waited to hear what was going on.

"It's pointing left, but we can't go left, it isn't possible." There were bushes and trees, but no trail towards the left. A.J. walked up to Tim and looked at the device.

"What does A.R. do?" A.J. asked Tim.

"I don't know, the old man didn't say anything about A.R." A.J. pressed the button that said A.R. on the train finder. The words alternate route appeared on the screen. The arrow pointed directly ahead.

"What did it do?" Benji asked.

"It wants us to continue straight, the way we've been going." Some of them moaned. "Come on guys we gotta go before....." They heard a loud horn.

"What does that mean?" Gloria asked.

"It's the cannibals, that's how they get together," Gibbs said. "The one that got away is probably calling for help."

"It's time to run," Tim said.

"I think that's a fair assessment." As they began running they saw cannibals in the trees above. Soon they were jumping out of the trees. Travis began shooting them, as the others with guns did the same thing.

"They are right behind us," Edward said.

"Who told you to look behind, keep going!," Tim said. Five cannibals snuck out of the bushes and one of them hit Tim in his face. He fell over, dropping the train finder. The same cannibal grabbed A.J. before she could fire her gun.

"Let me go!," A.J. said as she struggled to get free. He bit her under her right hand. When he looked up Michael hit him with the barrel of his gun.

"Bite that!," Michael said. Although they were surrounded, they continued to shoot at the cannibals. A.J., who was too hurt to shoot anyone sat down on the ground. Tim got up and began to look for the train finder. He started to panic when he didn't see it right away.

"I'm out," Edward said, referring to the bullets in his gun.

"I am too," Travis said. "But luckily I have this." He reached into his bag and pulled out a machine gun.

"Travis, why weren't you using that before?"

"I forgot I had it."

"Better late than never," Benji said. A huge net dropped down from the trees and covered all of them.

"I'll just shoot through." One of the cannibals grabbed one of the guns and knocked Travis in the head. With Travis unconscious they were able to grab his gun easily.

"Does anyone have any more ammo?" Tim asked.

"I'm out," Edward said.

"Me too," Benji said.

"Me three," Michael said.

"I had ammo in mine, but I can't get to my gun now," A.J. said.

"Can you get to your train finder?" Tim asked.

"Yeah." She reached for it.

"Not now, I just wanted to know."

"What do we do?" Mark asked.

"Not much we can do now, but wait."

"I know they don't expect to move this net with all of us in it," Edward said. They were shocked to see a cannibal that was 12 feet tall and 800 pounds. "Naaaw, me and my big mouth."

"Edward from now on shut up!," A.J. said.

"You guys have to remember you are no longer in your world," Gibbs said. "You are in a supernatural world where almost anything is possible." The giant cannibal walked to the net.

"Aye mack let us outta here," Edward said to the giant cannibal.

"Uhnnn, uhnnn," the giant cannibal said as he secured the net.

"Edward didn't I tell you to shut up?" A.J. asked meanly.

"Aye Mike you need to smack your girl, I would do it, but I don't believe in hitting broads," Edward said.

"You just too scared cause you know I would wup you."

"Guys please be quiet," Tim said.

"Thank you Tim," Benji said.

"You on the other hand Benji I will hit," Edward said. He smacked Benji in his face. Tim rolled his eyes.

"Uhnnn, uhnnn," the giant cannibal said. He attempted to lift the net.

"Oh no," Gloria said.

"I thought the van was uncomfortable, this looks like this is gonna make the van look like a dream trip," Benji said.

"That's if we don't suffocate each other," Tim said. The giant cannibal lifted the net and carried it like it was a bag. Although they were tight together, they knew immediately they wouldn't suffocate.

"Amazing," Gibbs said. The creature walked while he carried them. "This creature's strength is amazing."

"It is pretty amazing, I just wish we weren't the ones being carried," Gloria said.

"It feels funny," A.J. said, referring to the feeling of the giant cannibal walking with them.

"Not to me," Benji said. "It feels like I'm gonna throw up."

"Eeeeeeel!," many of them said.

"Benji if you did that it would make this walk however long it is a living hell," Tim said.

"This whole world is a living hell," Gloria said.

"Yes it is," Monica agreed.

"Where do you think he's taking us?" Michael asked Gibbs.

"Probably somewhere to eat," Gibbs said.

"Yay great, I could go for a little food." A.J. rolled her eyes at him as the net became very silent. "What, was it something I said?"

"No you idiot Gibbs means he's probably taking us somewhere where they will eat us," Edward said.

"Naaaaw, on 2nd thought, help, help, help!, Aye man I think I caught the wrong bus man, let me out!" The giant cannibal turned his head to the side.

"Hmmmm, hmmm, humnn," the giant cannibal said.

"Hnn, hnn, what does that mean, help, help!"

"It's no use Mike, who's gonna hear us?" Gloria asked.

"Be patient guys, if they don't eat us right away we'll have time to plan our escape," Tim said.

"That's a big if," Michael said.

"I'm with Michael on that one," A.J. said. "That's a big if."

"What happened?" Travis asked as he regained conciousness. "Where are we?" He looked at the giant cannibal. "Woe, that dude is huge, I can't believe he's actually carrying us."

"No one can," Gloria said.

"Where is he taking us?"

"We don't know T Money," Tim said.

"You aren't anxious to find out are you?" Edward asked.

"Yeah I actually am, if I'm gonna be eaten I would've kept my costume on." No one laughed at Travis' joke. "Ouch tough crowd."

"All we can do is wait," Tim said after taking a deep breath.

They were carried for an hour before the giant cannibal let them down. They fell to the ground hard.

"Couldn't he have warned us we were going down?" Travis asked.

"I guess not," Edward said as he saw the stars spinning all around him. They were in the net for hours, during this time period all but Tim and Gibbs fell asleep. One of the cannibals came up to the net and loosened it. Benji tried to get out, but was hit by a large stick the cannibal had.

"Benji!," Gloria yelled as the cannibal pulled her out of the net. Benji was dazed, but realized the cannibal was taking Gloria. Christopher cried as the cannibal dragged her out of the net.

"Where are you taking her, what are you gonna do to her, bring her back!," Benji demanded.

"Benji!"

"Gloria!" Benji got close to the opening of the net.

"Uhnnnuu, uhunuu!," the cannibal said. He hit Benji with the large stick which caused him to fall into A.J.'s legs. She had tears in her eyes as she saw Gloria being taken against her will.

"Mike," A.J. said, tearful. Michael hugged her. Benji felt like giving up, but Gloria was the coolest girl he had met in a while, hence his heart would not let him give up.

"We gotta get out of here," Benji told Tim. "The longer we wait the better chance they'll have of doing something awful to her."

"Tim?" Monica asked to see if he had any ideas. Tim was very upset and they could see all the pain in his face.

"I'm sorry guys, but this time I'm all out of ideas," Tim said. "Gibbs?"

"I may be able to get us out of here, but does anyone have a lighter?" Gibbs asked.

"I do, but I thought about burning the rope, but I may accidently burn us," Travis explained.

"No, no I'm not gonna do that." Travis handed Gibbs his lighter. "Now I know everyone's out of ammo, but do any of you still have your guns?"

"I do, " Edward said.

"Can I have it?"

"Sure." Edward, who wasn't that close to Gibbs, gave it to A.J. "Pass it." When it got to Gibbs he looked at the gun.

"I was hoping you would have a long gun, thanks."

"You welcome," Edward said, with a confused look on his face. He lit the front of the gun with the lighter.

"Now when you guys see one of those cannibals with the sharp spheres nearby let me know, until then I will continue to light this."

"There's one of them right now," Travis said.

"Mr. Dice would you make a lot of noise as you usually do?"

"Like what?" Benji asked.

"Anything to get his full attention and let me know when you have his full attention."

"O.k., hey you let me outta here, I wanna go home, you're so ugly yo mama tried to have an abortion after you were born!"

"Unnn-unn," the cannibal said.

"I think I got his attention, he's coming this way."

"Good, T Money hold the gun, but only hold it from here, unless you wanna get burnt that is," Gibbs said. Travis took the gun.

"What do you want me to do?, " Travis asked.

"Aim it through the net at the cannibal, you'll know what to do next."

"Unnn-uhhh!," the cannibal said when he got to the net. He grabbed the gun from Travis. "Ha, ha, ahhhhhhhhhhhh!" He dropped the sharp sphere.

"Mr. Dice grab the sphere."

"My pleasure," Benji said. He grabbed it and swung it at the cannibal. Once the sphere went into the cannibals back he screamed a little longer before falling down.

"That didn't help, we're still stuck in here," Travis said.

"Mr. Dice can you reach the sharp sphere?" Gibbs asked. Benji stretched and was able to pull it out of the cannibals back. "You can cut the rope with that, but only cut enough for one person to get out, we have to see where Gloria is first."

"I'll go," Benji said.

"Thought you would say that." Benji cut the rope and was on his way.

"Benji be careful," A.J. told him.

"I will," Benji said.

"Use the bushes to hide behind," Tim said. Benji nodded his head and then ran off. They were all nervous as they watched Benji leave their eyesight.

CHAPTER 12

Benji was gone for nearly ten minutes when he saw Gloria. She was tied up to a piece of wood. She was being guarded by two cannibals. There was a huge pot they were boiling. Benji was hiding behind a house made out of straws he assumed the cannibals made. He snuck inside the house.

"Ahuuua, ahuuuh," one of the cannibals said to the other.

"Ahhhhuhhhh, ahhhuhhh," the other one said. He walked away from the pot and went inside the straw house. Benji came from behind him and put a rope around the cannibal's neck and pulled until he passed out. He grabbed a machete and walked out of the house. The cannibal scratched Gloria's hand, causing her to bleed. She was crying in fear as the cannibal tasted her blood. He was excited after he swallowed it. He walked away from Gloria in order to grab the machete that was on the ground next to the pot. Gloria felt like crying, but instead closed her eyes. He lifted his hand up and walked closer to Gloria. He dropped the machete when his foot was pulled by a rope. Benji ran over to him as he was laying on the ground. Gloria peeked and was surprised to see Benji.

"Gloria shut your eyes," Benji said. He stabbed the cannibal in the back three times with the machete he got out of the house. He turned him over to make sure he was dead. When he didn't move, he ran over to Gloria and cut the rope that was holding her to the wood. She hugged Benji.

"Benji I didn't think I would see you again," Gloria told him.

"I wasn't gonna let you go that easy." They smiled at each other as they held each other's hands. Benji looked at the dead cannibal. "Sorry to spoil your dinner, but this is my lady." Benji and Gloria ran back to the others. When they made it back everyone's spirits were raised. "Now's the best time to go, most of them are not around."

"Then we'll go now," Tim said. He opened the net and got

out.

"There's one thing."

"And what is that?"

"There's a house up there that has weapons, I'm sure from humans like us they've captured over the years, I think we should get those weapons."

"Are you crazy, we should just get the hell out of here," Mark said.

"I agree with Mark, they may catch us again," Gloria said.

"It is dangerous I admit, but we need those weapons," Tim said. "We can't split up so we all have to go."

"I'm with you," Edward said.

"You know I am," Travis said.

"I would like a new gun," A.J. said.

"Then it's settled, we'll go," Tim said. Mark was upset, as he wiggled his way out of the net.

"Listen we could be killed going for those weapons," Mark said.

"And we could be killed escaping, at least with the weapons we have a better chance of escaping." Mark still didn't agree with Tim as Monica put her hand on his shoulder.

"Come on Mark, they've done a good job keeping us alive so far," Monica said.

"Yeah, I just hope it continues," Mark said.

"A.J., can I see your train finder?" Tim asked.

"Sure," A.J. said. She reached into her pocket, got it and gave it to Tim.

"Thanks." She nodded her head. "Good, a train station is in that direction, same way we wanna go."

"Let's go then," Travis said.

After they were all out of the net, they followed Benji to the house.

"Almost looks like a old native American house," Monica said.

"Alright here's how we'll do it," Tim said. "Me, Benji, and Michael will go inside the house and get some weapons."

"What about me?" Travis asked.

"I need you out here, just in case something happens, we won't be long." Tim, Benji and Michael went inside the house while the others stayed hidden in the bushes. When they walked in the house Benji opened the closet door where he got the machete from. Tim and Michael were surprised to see all the weapons. "We don't have a lot of time, so take the best ones."

"How are we gonna carry all these for the others?" Benji asked Tim, who hadn't thought of that. He was angry at himself for not thinking ahead.

"Damn, get everyone else in here." Benji began to run, but was stopped when Tim grabbed him by his arm. "Quietly and hurry up." Benji nodded his head and then left the straw house.

When all of them were inside the cannibal straw house, Tim handed all of the weapons out.

"A.J.," Tim said. She walked up to him and he gave her a simple hand gun. "T Money." Travis was handed a rifle.

"Yeah, I like this," Travis said.

"I knew you would." Tim smiled at him. "Ed." He gave Edward a rifle. "Mark, what would you like?"

"I like bow and arrows," Mark said. Tim handed Mark a bag full of arrows and the bow. "Thanks."

"Monica you want anything?" She shook her head.

"Baby at least take a gun."

"Yeah, I'll take a gun," Monica said.

"What kind?" Tim asked her.

"A small one will be alright." He handed her a small gun.

"Benji, I know you want this." Tim handed him a machete and Benji smiled at him. "Michael, I heard you liked knives." He handed Michael a belt with different sized knives on it.

"Thank you," Michael said.

"You welcome." Michael put the belt around his waist. "Gloria." She was about to say no when Tim lifted his hand up. She saw he was holding a small dagger. "This looks like something you could use." She took it from his hand.

"Yes it is," Gloria agreed. She smiled at Tim.

"And Gibbs."

"No thank you, you guys are all the protection I need," Gibbs said.

"Are you sure?"

"Yes, I am quite sure."

"O.k. I have extra ammo for all of our weapons too, well then let's go, quietly." Tim closed the closet and walked to the door that led outside. When he opened the door of the house he looked to see if he saw any of the cannibals. "I don't see any of them, but everyone take precaution, T Money you stay with Gibbs, he has to stay alive if we ever want to get home."

"You don't have to remind me of that," Travis said as he walked next to Gibbs. All of them walked out of the house quietly and carefully. Tim pulled out the train finder. After walking for 10 minutes, the trail broke up.

"Which way?" A.J. asked.

"It says make a right," Tim said. They followed him as he walked towards the rightside of the trail. Five cannibals found the cannibal Benji killed by the pot and began screaming. One of them pulled out a horn and blew into it. The strangers from a parallel dimension froze when they heard the horn. They all looked nervously thinking about dying if they got caught again. Tim realized he had to say something to break everyone out of their trance. "Run!" They all began running. After running for a while they began to hear the cannibals moving in the bushes. One of them jumped out of the bushes and pushed Edward down. He punched the cannibal off of him and then Travis shot him. Travis helped Edward to his feet. Mark turned around and could see some of them running towards him. When he looked up he saw some of the cannibals were in the trees.

Mark aimed his bow and arrow and fired at one of them as he ran. His arrow connected with the cannibal, causing him to fall down from the tree. Mark grabbed another arrow and was able to kill two more cannibals as he continued to run. They saw the trail was coming to an end. "The arrow on the train finder is blinking, that means we are real close." Five cannibals jumped in front of the opening in the woods. One of the cannibals was a girl with a whip in her hand. She whipped it at Tim before he could get his gun out. He dropped his gun and the train finder. Gibbs went to retrieve it, but one of the cannibals tried to kill him with his spiked bat. Travis shot him three times until he fell. A.J. shot the girl in the face as she was on top of Tim, choking him. Once the bullet connected with her she fell backwards. Edward shot the last two cannibals as Gibbs handed Tim back the train finder. Travis gave Tim his gun back. "Thank you." The cannibals behind them were coming closer. The visitors ran out of the woods into a playground. They saw an opening that they could tell led underground. "We're almost there." He stopped running.

"Tim what are you doing?" A.J. asked. The others ran in front of Tim.

"What are you doing Tim?" Travis asked, as he and Gibbs ran towards the underground entrance.

"I hate to do this A.J., but," Tim said.

"What?" A.J. asked, dumbfounded. He scratched the scar on her right arm. "Ahhhh!" Michael ran over to Tim and pushed him.

"Why'd you do that?" Michael asked meanly.

"We need blood to enter, remember?" Tim asked. Michael smiled at Tim. A cannibal came rushing at them. Michael threw a knife into his forehead, making him hit the ground. They ran towards the entrance, Michael was holding A.J.'s bleeding scar under her right hand. Cannibals were still running after them and they were closer than before. When they got to the stairs they saw the door.

"Why won't it open?" Edward asked.

"It needs my blood," A.J. said. Michael walked her over to the plate in the wall.

"Tim, take Gibbs, I'll guard the door," Travis said.

"I'll help," Edward said. A.J. put her right wrist on the plate and the plate flashed.

"You are human, you have 2 minutes to come through the door," they heard a voice from the plate say. The door began to open as Travis and Edward shot at the cannibals as they came down the stairs. When the door was all the way open A.J. and Michael were the first to go in. Tim looked at Mark and Monica.

"Go!," he yelled. They ran inside the door. "Chris, Gloria, come on!" They ran through the door. "Benji!" Benji looked back at Travis and Edward. "Don't worry, I'll make sure they get inside." Benji ran in. "Come on wrap it up guys!" Edward and Travis walked backwards as they continued to fire. "Gibbs I'm right behind you, when you get in there stay with Benji." Tim pushed Gibbs into the train station. They didn't see any more cannibals come down the stairs. Tim turned his back and walked inside. Edward and Travis smiled at each other, they were relieved. As they were walking to the opening of the train station they heard noise coming from the stairs. They were almost afraid to look. When they turned around they were stunned to see the giant cannibal had slid down the stairs. He had to duck his head to fit. They raised their guns, but he immediately knocked the guns out of their hands.

"Shoot!," Travis said.

"Shoot is right," Edward said.

"Uhnnn, uhnnn!," the giant cannibal said as he swung at them. They dodged his hits and ran to the opening of the wall.

"Hurry up!," Tim yelled, as the door was starting to shut. Travis went through without any problems, but Edward had to turn sideways to fit. The giant cannibal held the door open as it was about to shut and then pushed it back open.

"Warning, warning, malfunction, system malfunction," the voice from the plate said.

"Uuuhhhh!," the giant cannibal said before smashing the plate with his bare hands. Edward, Tim and Travis were shocked to see him bust through the entrance. His head went through the concrete wall.

"Wow, you know how much that would hurt a regular person?" Travis asked Edward and Tim.

"Yeah, but he's not a regular person," Edward said.

"Sure isn't," Tim said as he aimed his gun at him. People in the train station were screaming as they saw the giant cannibal. He picked up a lady and threw her through the glass of a bookstore inside the train station. Mark began hitting him with arrows from his bow, while Tim shot him with his gun. He picked up a mailbox and threw it at another man who was shooting at him.

"I have an idea," Mark said. "T Money."

"Yeah?" Travis asked.

"You still have that lighter?"

"Yeah."

"Let me see it." Travis handed the lighter to Mark. Mark lit his arrow and fired it at the giant cannibals face, causing him to flinch when the arrow hit his face. Everyone at the train station with a gun in the vicinity shot at his face. The fire spread until his whole face was on fire.

"Ahualll, ahualll, ahuall!," the giant cannibal screamed. He fell face first to the ground. One of the security guards at the train station looked over at Tim and his friends.

"You guys didn't tell me you were gonna invite him," he said with a smile on his face.

"I hate party crashers," Michael said.

"Where you guys going?"

"To Los Angeles," Tim said.

"Oh, go that way." The security guard pointed to his right. "The signs will tell you what train to get on."

"Thank you sir."

"You welcome."

"Good shot Mark."

"Thanks," Mark said.

"I think you are officially a part of the team now," Travis said.

"Now aren't you glad we went back for the weapons?" Benji asked. Mark smiled and nodded his head. While the security guard called for help they walked to an escalator. It took them down a floor where they saw a sign that said Los Angeles. When they got to the train platform they were surprised to see the train was already there. As they entered the train they felt excitement, they knew they were one step closer to going home. When they sat down Gibbs could tell A.J.'s arm was hurting her.

"How you holding up A.J.?" Michael asked.

"Still hurts," A.J. said. Gibbs got out of his seat and walked over to Michael and A.J.

"I'm gonna see where they have the first aid kit at," Gibbs said.

"First aid kit?" Michael asked.

"After the world died all the trains on the new underground railroad were required to have them on trains, I'll be back with something for you."

"Thank you." When Gibbs returned he had peroxide, ointment and a band-aid.

"Excuse me Michael." Michael, who was sitting next to A.J. moved over a seat and allowed Gibbs to sit next to her. He poured the peroxide on her bite. After it dried up he rubbed ointment on it and then put a band-aid on it.

"Gibbs," A.J. said, looking at him with a worried expression.

"What is it honey?"

"Am I gonna turn into a zombie?"

"No, no dear, you were bit by a cannibal, however when we get to my house I will give you a tetanus shot, I don't want it to become infected."

"Thank you Gibbs."

"You welcome." Gibbs got off the seat and moved back to his previous seat, while Michael moved back next to A.J. As soon as he put his hand around her shoulder, she put her head on it.

"How long is this train ride gonna be?" Tim asked.

"4 to 6 hours depending on how many stops this train makes."

"4 to 6 hours?" Edward asked loudly.

"Yes, L.A. is the end of the line."

"That's too long, what if we have to pee?" Travis asked.

"They have bathrooms on these trains."

"Where?" Mark asked as he stood up.

"Uhh, can't seem to remember."

"What you looking for man?" one of the passengers asked Mark.

"The bathroom."

"2nd to last car, hope you can hold it though, this is a long train, you have a lot of cars to go through."

"Yeah alright, thanks." He looked at Monica. "I'll be right back." He walked to the bathroom. Edward and Benji noticed the man was Edwin. Michael and A.J. were asleep.

"Aye Edwin," Edward said with a big smile on his face.

"Who are you guys?" Edwin asked Edward and Benji. "And how do you know my name?"

"We almost didn't know it was you with that big fro," Benji said.

"I still don't know who you guys are and as far as the fro I've had this for years." Edward and Benji looked at each other, they both realized it was the Edwin of the dimension they were currently in.

"Oh sorry," Edward said.

"Yeah we thought you were another Edwin," Benji said. "You look a lot like him."

"Please no one looks this good," Edwin said. They smiled at him. "But while we talking I would like to interest you in purchasing these two guns." He pulled out two brand new guns. "They haven't been fired yet." He opened the guns and showed them the bullets. "Silver bullets, these guns are made specifically for werewolves, if you have a werewolf problem." He aimed the gun at the window as if he were going to fire it. "Baaaw, not anymore, so what do you say?"

"How can we purchase it, we have no money," Edward said.

"Who said anything about money, we haven't used cash since the end of the world."

"Then what do you use?"

"Food, I take candy, well only if it's good, clothes and I also take old weapons for new ones."

"I already got silver bullets, but I like that gun," Tim, who was listening to Edwin said.

"It's important to have the right gun for it, this gun was made to kill werewolves."

"I have this gun," Tim said, handing Edwin his gun.

"I like it." Edwin gave Tim the gun that fired silver bullets.

"It's yours."

"Thank you."

"Pleasure doing business with you, you expecting werewolves."

"Maybe, always best to be prepared.

"In this world, yeah." Tim looked at Gibbs, who was a few seats away from him.

"Gibbs how long were you in there?"

"It was, it was, I can't seem to remember, that's odd. How could I forget a thing like that?" Gibbs asked.

"Where was he?" Edwin asked Tim.

"In Homicidal Asylum," Tim said. Edwin's eyes grew big.

"What, you got him out of there."

"Yeah, all of us did."

"You get props on that, no one makes it out of there alive, I lost a few friends in there."

"We had some connects."

"Well if he was in there he may of had his mind blocked by a evil wizard."

"You're right, I do happen to remember meeting a wizard, but I can't recall his name," Gibbs said. Tim looked at Gibbs and then he turned back to Edwin.

"What can a wizard do to him?" Tim asked.

"Anything you can imagine man, but this sounds like a simple spell, the wizard made him forget important information. Wow though, he must be pretty important if a wizard blocked his mind. They must be scared of him or he did something to piss them off, either way he's important. I see why you risked your life to get him out," Edwin said, before standing up. "Alright well I'm about to go to another car, are you guys interested in playing cards?" Tim looked around the train car and noticed he, Travis, Edward, Gibbs, Benji and Monica were the only ones awake.

"Uhh, not right now, maybe later, I am hungry though."

"No you mean we are hungry," Benji said.

"What about you Monica?"

"I could go for some food," Monica said.

"That's close to the bathroom, they have food in one of the cars, not as far as the bathroom though," Edwin told them.

"Thanks, and one last thing," Tim said.

"Yeah, what is it?"

"How do you break a spell?"

"Kill the wizard or have him reverse the spell." Tim looked down, thinking about what Edwin told him. "Alright guys have a nice day." They said goodbye to Edwin as he exited the car.

"We gotta get that spell off, we need to know the truth," Tim told Edward.

"But first we have to eat," Edward said.

"You are right my friend." Tim stood up out of his seat. "Monica you coming?"

"In a minute, I'ma wait for Mark to come back."

"O.k."

CHAPTER 13

When Mark and Monica arrived at the food car they were surprised at how it looked. It was a little restaurant where they saw people eating at the tables with their guns sticking out of their back. Tim smiled when he saw them walk in.

"You guys gonna eat here?" Tim asked, holding his food in a container.

"It doesn't matter," Monica said.

"You guys can stay here, Benji and Edward are here, I'm just going back because I don't want them to freak out when they wake up and don't see any of us. It isn't that many people on this train, is Gibbs asleep?"

"Yeah, he's knocked out, they all are, I'm surprised I'm not. It was a crazy last two days. I thought last night was crazy, but today was even crazier, escaping from those creatures and then the cannibals, no one will ever believe us back home."

"Never," Mark agreed.

"You'll just have a good story to tell your kids one day," Tim said, smiling.

"Are you sure you don't wanna eat in here, me and Mark can go back and stay with the others," Monica said.

"No, enjoy yourself, you guys haven't had that much time for that lately."

"Thanks, Tim you're a good guy," Mark said.

"Thank you." Tim smiled and then left the food car.

"If it wasn't for that guy right there we would be dead."

"All of them Mark, they all saved our lives in the asylum and we helped save their lives too," Monica said. "But I get what you're saying, Tim takes a lot of the responsibility of looking after everyone on his hands."

"Maybe since he's older than us he feels that need to be responsible for us."

"Maybe, but he's only a grade ahead of us, he's a freshman at Wilson, I heard." Mark nodded his head as they walked to an empty table across from Edward and Benji. Mark was stunned when he looked to his left and saw one of the twins that saved his and Monica's life the night before. He was still wearing his pirate Halloween costume.

"Walter!" The twin turned to Mark.

"I'm Wally, what's up, I thought you were dead," Wally said. They stood up and hugged each other.

"I thought you and your brother were dead."

"My brother was stabbed, but he's still alive."

"What happened?"

"We ran into some K.B.G.'S."

"K.B.G.'S, what's that?"

"Killer biker gang, they are bikers that kill people for fun. My brother and I were fighting them when he was stabbed."

"Where is your brother now?"

"In a local hospital, well local to me. It's underground, next to one of the train stations, I get off in two stops. He asked for some real food, he didn't like the hospital food too much." Wally laughed thinking about his brother, Walter.

"Killer biker gang, no we didn't run into any of them."

"Good you don't want to, they aren't even human."

"Are they Camadeians?"

"What's that?"

"Now you don't wanna know."

"These things are green, they look like frogs, they're hard to kill because there stomach can't be penetrated by a gun or a knife or anything. You have to shoot them in the head or mouth or decapitate them." He pulled out his sword. "That's what I did, but anyway after we got separated last night what happened to you and your girl?"

"We were taken as lab rats to some insane asylum where the doctors are insane and most of the patients are regular. They were aliens too, we were lucky. You remember that guy with the storm trooper outfit?"

"Yeah, I think he goes to my school."

"Yeah, he and a few others saved me and Monica's life."

"Where are you going to now?"

"L.A."

"Should be pretty safe, heard it is very low on zombies."

"How do you know so much?"

"I've met a lot of the brass in this area. If you wanna stay with us you are more than welcomed."

"No we're going home."

"How?"

"We found Professor Gibbs."

"Good luck at getting his help, he sent us here to die."

"No, Professor Gibbs of this world."

"He must be a lot better than the Professor Gibbs from back home."

"Yeah, he's like his good twin." Being that Wally is a twin he laughed. "Are you gonna come with us?"

"I can't leave my brother, and he is in no condition to travel."

"You really don't look like you wanna leave though."

"I can't lie, I will miss my parents. I do feel a peace with the people I met in this chaotic world, as weird as that sounds. I feel more comfortable with the people in this world than I do with the people back home."

"I know what you mean, I never would've imagined myself being good friends with a 6th grader or a freshman, but we all feel like family and after this is all done they will be my best friends forever."

"Then you can see why I'm gonna stay."

"Yeah I can, it's just so dangerous here."

"Yeah but we are doing big things and we plan on sending all the evil back to hell and I wanna be alive to see it."

"Well o.k., it doesn't look like I'm gonna convince you to go with us." They shook hands.

"Well I'm going back to the car where I was sitting at, good luck Mark."

"Good luck to you too." He walked out of the car. Mark walked back to the table Monica was sitting at.

"I heard him say he wasn't going with us?" Monica said.

"Nope, he's staying."

"What is he crazy?"

"No, it's his decision, I just hope it's the right one."

Although it was a long trip to L.A., the N.T.S. and their new friends were happy for the relaxation. While they were on the train they were told they could rent a vehicle from the train station. People going to the train stations would leave vehicles there all the time, so they were always available for new drivers. Some of the train stations did not provide that resource, but many did. No one on this world wanted to be dropped off in the middle of nowhere and have to walk on foot. When they got off the train they decided to rent a van. By the time they left the train station parking garage it was night in L.A. Tim was driving the van as the others looked out the windows in disbelief.

"Wow I thought our L.A. was dirty," Benji said.

"It looks like riots went down here," Travis said.

"Zombies, werewolves, K.B.G.'s, almost everything but riots," Gibbs said. Many of the street lights were smashed and some of the skyscrapers had no lights.

"Man I have to turn on the brights just to see out here," Tim said as he turned on the bright lights of the van.

"Look at the buildings downtown, they look so dead," Michael said.

"Gloria where did everybody go?" Christopher asked.

"I don't know baby," Gloria answered.

"Turn right here," Gibbs said. "At the next intersection turn right, then after the next two lights pull over, I'll show you where."

"I'm surprised you can still remember where you live," Tim said.

"Yeah, the other Gibbs didn't live where you do," Edward said. Gibbs was quiet.

"What's wrong Gibbs?" Gloria asked.

"Something is still wrong," Gibbs said.

"Your memory."

"Yes, the other Gibbs should've lived in L.A. too."

"But he didn't, he lived on Linden Avenue."

"Yes and something is wrong with that, but I can't remember what."

"That wizard must have a powerful lock on you," Benji said.

"He made me forget important things."

"I know, that's why we're surprised you can still remember your way home," Tim said.

"Yes, now why is that?" Gibbs tried to understand, but couldn't.

"Just rest Gibbs, until we figure out a way to break the spell you're never gonna remember," Gloria said.

"You're right, you're right."

When they got to Gibbs house they were cautious. Edward and Travis had their guns drawn as they walked into his house. When they turned the lights on Tim, Edward and Travis searched the house for intruders.

"No it looks like we're o.k.," Tim said. Edward handed A.J. back her gun, but she didn't accept it.

"Even though I feel weird without it you can keep it," A.J. told Edward. "I never thought I would feel weird without a gun."

"Don't worry A.J. I may have extra weapons in here somewhere," Gibbs said.

"Good cause every time I get a big gun I get it taken away," Travis, who was using Monica's gun said. "No offense Monica."

"None taken, I hate guns, you can use mine all you want until you get a big gun," Monica said.

"I just wanna know what room is that machine in," Edward said.

"Should be in here," Gibbs said. He walked to the room where the machine was as the others followed him. When they got inside they saw a junky room with two big machines and two paintings. Gibbs tried to turn on the dimensional machine but it wouldn't turn on.

"All the power should be working," Tim said.

"Are you sure it's plugged up?" A.J. asked. Tim looked at the connection.

"No, it's connected." Tim continued to examine the machine. "Looks like a piece is missing."

"But why would a piece be missing?" Benji asked.

"I don't know, but somewhere in his mind he knows." Tim pointed to Gibbs. A.J. walked up to him.

"Professor Gibbs think, please think," A.J. begged him.

"Yes, yes, yes, I'm thinking," Gibbs said. "That's it."

"What?" most of the people in the room asked.

"I took a piece out."

"But why?" A.J. asked.

"Someone wanted to take this machine and use it."

"You mean like the other professor Gibbs did?" Travis asked.

"I see what T Money is getting at," Tim said.

"What?" Gloria asked.

"The Professor Gibbs of our world sent us here, but someone from this world was trying to go to our world."

"Yes, I just can't remember who, but I do recall hiding the missing piece somewhere in this room," Gibbs said. All but Christopher looked around the room with their eyes.

"We have to look around." Everyone except Christopher began searching the room.

"I didn't find the piece, but I found this," A.J. said, holding an empty bottle.

"Amnesia potion," Edward said, reading the bottle.

"That must be why you can't remember anything, someone must've forced you to drink that," Mark said.

"No, no, no I drunk that myself, I remember that," Gibbs said.

"But why?" Gloria asked.

"They wanted me to show them how to work this machine, but I refused."

"Who?"

"I can't remember to be honest, I can't even remember how to work this machine myself."

"Great, we're stuck here," Edward said.

"Not necessarily my friends, I kept a journal of this machine, that too is somewhere in here, if only I could remember."

"They're probably together, keep searching," Tim told everyone as he too looked through every item in the room.

"In the movies people always hide things in paintings," Michael said.

"He's right," Edward said, looking at the two paintings in the room. "Mike let me see one of your knives."

"Sure thing." Michael handed Edward one of his knives.

"Which one should I cut open first?"

"Try the picture of my daughter," Gibbs said.

"Wait Gibbs this beautiful girl in this picture is your daughter?" A.J. asked.

"Yes."

"Where is she?"

"I unfortunately can't seem to recall that either." Everyone in the room looked sad.

"Don't worry about it," A.J. said as she smiled at Gibbs. Edward grabbed the painting off the wall, cut through it and found the journal.

"Walla!," Edward said. Everyone in the room became excited. A.J. hugged Edward before running over to Michael.

"You're a genius Mike!" She kissed him on his cheek, making him blush.

"It's book marked on a page."

"Maybe that's the page that it needs to be on," Tim said. Tim and Edward turned the journal together. They were happy that the page was book marked with the missing part. "We have this too." Tim held up the missing part in order for everyone in the room to see. Most of the people in the room were so excited they cheered, screamed, hugged and laughed.

"How long are you gonna need to fix it?"

"Well, first I need the piece and my journal," Gibbs said.

"Sorry," Tim said before handing the journal to Gibbs.

"Quite alright, you are excited which you should be, you're all going home." Gibbs skimmed through the journal. "It shouldn't take me too long, just give me an hour in here alone and it should be ready." They smiled as they listened to Gibbs tell them that.

"A.J. I do need to attend to your injury."

"I was hoping you forgot, I hate shots," A.J. said.

"Don't worry, it'll only sting for a second."

"Can Mike stay in here with me?"

"Sure." Michael walked next to A.J. as the others left the room.

CHAPTER 14

After an hour passed Gibbs called all of them back into the room.

"My friends the machine is back and working," Gibbs said. They all became excited. "I have to enter a code just for it to work proper, the code is probably what they wanted. Once you have the code, if you study this machine long enough, you'll know how to work it."

"So how does it work?" Tim asked.

"After you put in the code all these buttons represent different dimensions. You type in the one you wanna go to, type set and then go, the machine asks you if you are sure, you push yes and then the gateway opens up and you are there."

"How are we ever gonna find ours?" A.J. asked.

"She's right," Tim said. "There could be hundreds of different dimensions, maybe even thousands."

"Your dimension is 128907," Gibbs said.

"But how do you know?" A.J. asked. Gibbs took a deep breath.

"My mind is just telling me that it is, don't ask me how I know, I just do."

"That's good enough for me, are you guys ready to go?" Edward asked. They all responded positively.

"You guys what about Dracula, shouldn't we tell him we arrived safely and that we're about to go home?" Gloria asked. Most of the people in the room agreed.

"Dracula is your friend," Gibbs heard in his head.

"Yes, Dracula is my friend," Gibbs said, which caused A.J. to look at him and worry. Michael noticed the concern look on A.J.'s face.

"What's wrong kid?" Michael asked her.

"Every time Dracula's mentioned Gibbs says he's his friend," A.J. said.

"So."

"Yeah he's our friend too," Travis said.

"A.J. if it weren't for him we wouldn't of made it today," Gloria said.

"No, we made it because of us, all of you, yes they gave us weapons and disguises, but we have a strong team. Getting out of that hospital was no joke, we did it, not Count Dracula." Everyone in the room was quiet. A.J. turned her head away from them and looked at the machine. Gibbs programmed the machine to their dimension.

"Well it was nice meeting all of you," Gibbs said. "I need you to stand here." He pointed to the right of the machine. "It will take everything from this side."

"Gibbs what does that red button do?" A.J. asked, pointing to the large red button on the dimensional machine.

"That's for transporting a whole world to a different world."

"But what would you need to do that for?" Tim asked.

"Say a virus breaks out and thousands are dying from it, I could transport all the people from that Earth to a Earth where the same disease or virus has been cured for years or if a asteroid is going to wipe out the Earth I would be able to transfer all the people."

"How long?" A.J. asked.

"In an hour."

"An hour sounds great," Dracula said. They were shocked to see him and some of the people in the room were so startled they nearly jumped. "Oh I'm sorry to startle you, I did knock though, I thought you might be in trouble. The door was unlocked so I just came in."

"What do you mean by an hour sounds great?" Tim asked.

"This!" He pushed Gibbs down and pressed the red button.

"No!," some of the people in the room said, while others were too shocked or caught off guard to say or do anything. They saw Theodore walk into the room with a big grin on his face.

"You double crosser!," Benji yelled.

"Of course, how else could I have got to your world, all the humans to eat," Dracula said.

"I thought you said your rule was never attack humans?" Tim asked as he reached into his pocket.

106

"That is my rule never attack humans, convert them or kill them." Dracula had an evil look in his eyes. As Dracula laughed, the visitors from the parallel world could feel they were getting ready to be transported.

"Laugh this off!" Tim sprayed his garlic spray in Dracula's mouth, causing him to begin choking, eventually falling to the floor of the room. Theodore transformed into a werewolf and leaped at all of them, causing everyone to scream. Most of them closed their eyes, but when they reopened them they were in a quiet neighborhood. "We made it back."

"Just in time too," Michael said. Tim turned around and saw Gibbs was unconscious.

"Gibbs!" Tim and Michael ran to him. "Gibbs what's wrong?" Tim asked as he lifted his head off of the ground.

"Must get in doors," Gibbs said, before coughing two times. "All the people the other Gibbs transported to the nightmare world will come back here first, this is their home dimension, the machine will recognize their DNA and send them back first, after they are all here the machine will start sending every living being from the nightmare world here, ahhhhh!"

"What's wrong?" Edward asked.

"Memory coming back, take me home."

"We can't, remember the other Gibbs is there."

"No, take me back to the same house we came from in other dimension, that's my real home." Ten more people appeared on the street, all of them were zombies that were human the last time they were on the world. Tim and his friends saw them.

"We gotta go now!," Travis yelled as the zombies ran towards them. Travis shot one in the head. After Edward shot one in the head, five more zombies appeared on the street. "Shoot, Edward cover me, A.J.!" Travis threw A.J. his gun. Travis ran to a pickup truck he saw in a driveway, but was chased by two zombies. A.J. and Edward fired at them. Travis kicked the closest one to him into the other one, making them both fall. He grabbed a brick and smashed the pickup truck window. "I can't wait until I get back to driving cars again." He unlocked the door as A.J. killed one of the zombies. Travis hot-wired the pickup truck once he was inside it. A light in the house came on as Travis put the pickup truck in reverse, running over some of the zombies as more appeared on the street. "Get in!" Benji cut off a zombie's head with his machete, before jumping on the back of the pickup truck. All of them got into the back of the pickup truck while holding off the zombies with their weapons.

Mark hit a zombie in the head with a bow and arrow before making his way to the pickup truck. As he was getting on a zombie bit his leg.

"Ahhhhhh!," Mark screamed.

"Mark!," Monica yelled. Edward shot the zombie in the head three times.

"Hey what are you doing with my truck?" the neighbor asked. Edward looked at the man as the zombie fell to the ground.

"Leaving, and I suggest you do the same," Edward said. He got in on the passenger's side and shut the door.

"It's my truck, I'm not leaving till I get it back." He tried to chase after them as Travis drove away. He became scared when he saw the zombies. "Oh my god!" He tried to run back inside his house, but ten more zombies appeared in front of him. They began feeding on him. "Ahhhhhhhh, no, no, no, ahhhhhh, help, ahhhhhhh!"

When they got to Gibbs house, which was a mirror image of the house they had been in on the other world, they felt very confused. They didn't understand why the evil Professor Gibbs had two houses and how Gibbs knew about it. They hoped their questions would be answered soon.

"Someone's been here recently," Gloria said.

"How do you know?" Tim asked.

"Someone recently washed those dishes." She pointed to the clean dishes on the counter.

"It was Professor Gibbs, that probably wasn't even his real house, the house he held us at."

"What do you mean?" Benji asked.

"He means the other Gibbs probably killed whoever stayed in that house, he's evil," Gibbs said.

"How do you know?" Michael asked.

"Help me sit down." A.J. who was holding him, helped him to the couch as Monica helped Mark to one of the chairs.

"Alright Gibbs, start from the beginning," Edward said.

"The beginning?"

"The very beginning."

"O.k. from the start the nightmare world was bad, a lot of hateful people, if you read through their history books, but the real nightmare started when the Book of Evil was opened."

"Book of Evil, what's that?"

"The Book of Evil, also known by its other name, The Devil's Book. It's said the book was opened by a man by the name of Jesus Tomas Khan. It is said that Khan searched the whole world looking for this book, he had twenty or more people with him looking for this book."

"But why was he interested in it?" Benji asked.

"A evil man many believed to be Satan himself had visited him one night and told him if he wanted power he needed to possess that book. In 1966 he and his team found it. As soon as he saw the book he realized it was sealed. Only someone naive or with a heart of darkness could open that book up when it's sealed. He was able to cut the seal with his bare hands. He opened the book and was possessed by it instantly. As soon as it was open all the evil things in the book came out."

"How long was the book open?" Michael asked.

"About two minutes, but evil moves fast, some of the evil in that book possessed people, some of the evil turned into vampires, some of the evil turned into plagues. His men tried to pull him away from the book, but were unsuccessful the first two times. When they got him to close the book, he was insane, he tried to open the book again, but was shot."

"How did they destroy the book?" Travis asked.

"They didn't."

"Then where is it?" A.J. asked.

"No one knows."

"I would've burned it," Benji said.

"It can't be destroyed like that, only by the blood of Jesus

Christ can it be destroyed. The men buried it somewhere and took an oath never to discuss it again, for if they did and it fell into the wrong hands the world would not be able to manage. The book was only open for two minutes, just imagine if someone had it open for five or for ten minutes, or for an hour." All of the young men and women listening to Gibbs story were afraid. "I was in the nightmare world for two years."

"Two years?"

"Yes my friends, I am the true Professor Gibbs of this world." Some of them had shocked expressions on their faces, while others smiled.

"Of course, the other Professor Gibbs is so evil because he's from the nightmare world," Tim said.

"Yes, that is right Tim, the wizard Theodamordeous made me forget. When I came to the nightmare world humans were catching up with them, they found better ways of hiding and communicating. When Professor Gibbs realized I was his alternate from a parallel world he smashed my laptop and traded places with me."

"What was the laptop for?" Edward asked.

"That's how I got back."

"You had a way of coming back to your world after visiting another?" Tim asked.

"Yes, I was looking for a cure for all cancers, my wife at the time was ill with the disease, after she passed I continued looking. When I got stranded on that world the Count wanted to know how to get to my world. I had already found my counterpart's house and saw his machine, identical to mine. I took one of the pieces out, hid the journal he wrote behind the painting and drunk the amnesia potion. When the Count, Theodore and Theodamordeous came they were upset. He said if you really don't wanna remember I'll make you forget everything and I did, but he made me remember Dracula is my friend even though he wasn't my friend. He had me committed to Homicidal Asylum and made me tell them everything I remembered. Since I thought he was my friend I couldn't shut up about this Earth, he made me forget this was my true home, he made me think this was a world I visited, when it was the nightmare world

I visited."

"What happened to your daughter?" A.J. asked.

"I wish I knew, but I did tell her if I don't come back when I'm supposed to, leave. I had extra money locked away in a safe, she had the extra key."

"Now all the evil is coming here, what are we gonna do?" Mark asked as he continued to feel pain in his leg. "If you have any tricks let me know, if not after I die I'ma zombie."

"Mark don't say that," Monica said.

"It's the truth baby."

"Gibbs can't we stop this?" Tim asked.

"It's already started, just like The Book of Evil contaminated the world in only two minutes, this is the same," Gibbs said.

"No, this is worst, every living being evil or good is being transported here, how can we stop it?"

"I'm telling you we can't."

"So what are you telling me, we are gonna sit here and die?"

"No, we can't stop it now, but we can get to it before it ever happens."

"I don't get it, I'm confused."

"Me too," Gloria said.

"Gibbs are you sure your mind is back?" Edward asked.

"Yes, I created a time machine while I was here," Gibbs told them.

"The other machine next to the dimensional machine," Tim said.

"I forgot about that, the other Gibbs threatened to take us back to the dino days, saying we would be eaten by a T-Rex," said Michael.

"We have to get to his house and use the time machine."

"I still don't see how going in the past is gonna help us," A.J. said.

"The only way that it will is if we get to the basement..."

"Basement before Professor Gibbs presses the dimensional machine and sends us to the nightmare world," Tim said, cutting off Gibbs.

"That's right."

"So it'll be like we never left."

"That's it."

"So you're saying we have to fight through vampires, zombies, werewolves, aliens and Professor Gibbs just to get to the time machine to go back in time and stop the same Professor from sending us to the nightmare world?" asked Travis.

"Yes."

"O.k., I'm down."

"I'm sorry all I have is knives, each of you without a weapon take a knife." A.J. and Monica went to the kitchen to get knives. All of them who remained in the room heard a scream. Edward, Michael and Tim ran into the kitchen in order to see why Monica or A.J. screamed. When they got in the kitchen they saw Monica lying on the floor with the door leading outside open.

"Why'd you scream?" Edward asked Monica as he helped her to her feet.

"And where's A.J.?" Michael asked, as the others made their way into the kitchen.

"That wasn't me screaming, that was A.J., something or someone knocked me off my feet."

"We gotta go outside," Tim told Edward. He nodded his head and he, Michael and the rest of the group followed Tim outside. They didn't see anyone in the back, but when they got to the front of the house they saw Dracula holding A.J. by her neck in the grass.

"Stop in your tracks or I will bite her," Dracula said. Everyone was frozen.

"Why were you so interested in getting to our world?" Gloria asked.

"Humans you kill and destroy each other all the time, but in a time of need you all stick together and fight the greater enemy. The humans of my world have turned into smart soldiers, in 40 years or a little less they would have destroyed most of the vampires. They already had garlic filled train stations, they would of gotten rid of the werewolves and all the aliens, but here we have a 2nd chance, this could last forever here."

"Not if I can help it," Tim said as he pointed his gun at Dracula.

"Easy Tim, you don't want me to hurt her, right Michael." Michael was scared, not for himself, but he was afraid Count Dracula was going to kill A.J.

"Just leave her alone!," Michael said. Count Dracula cut A.J.'s neck with his nail. Once it bled a little he put his finger on it and licked it from his finger.

"Tasty, I didn't introduce you to my brides." Three beautiful women dressed in white came out of the darkness. Behind them they saw Theodore walk up with a cold hearted smile.

"Oh so you lied about that too, saying your wives were dead," Travis said, holding his gun at Dracula.

"I didn't lie T Money, in you humans' concept of death they did die."

"But he brought us back," one of them said.

"Me and my sisters never had this much fun when we were alive," another one of them said.

"Yeah, I feel more alive than I've ever felt," one of them said as she grinded against Tim.

"Wow they are beautiful," Benji said, causing Gloria to roll her eyes.

"Beautiful and dangerous," Gloria said.

"Of course, that's the way I love my women."

"What did you do with Frankenstein's monster?" Tim asked.

"He didn't like it when we told him we were gonna kill all of you, he's taken a fondness to all of you," Theodore said.

"Yes, he actually tried to attack us," Dracula said.

"I had to tie him up in chains." Theodore pointed to a tree behind him where they could see Frankenstein's monster was tied up and bleeding from the left side of his face.

"That was mean, he thought you were his friends," Gloria said. "Well we thought you were our friends too."

"You are, cause you led us here," Dracula said. Dracula, his brides and Theodore began laughing.

"Your breath stinks," A.J. said. Although Dracula was holding her with his arm around her neck, she was able to get her right hand free and spray the garlic spray at him. She was trying to spray him in his mouth, however she sprayed him in his eyes by accident. When the spray went in his eyes he was in so much pain he let her go immediately.

"Ahhhhhhh, kill them all, kill them all!" Theodore took off his shirt and threw it to the ground.

"I like you Edward, but now you have to die!," Theodore said to him.

"Naaaw!," Edward said, before running. Dracula's brides were showing all of them their teeth.

"Hey Gloria you wanna help me kill these broads?" A.J. asked.

"Yeah, I don't want people reading to think I'm the pretty girl in the story that never fights," Gloria said.

"Well that's what you are."

"A.J. shut up girl." Gloria smiled.

"Coming Monica?"

"Yeah, I fought those things at the hospital, these little girls shouldn't be hard," Monica said.

"Christopher stay on the porch and if you get scared run in the house and hide," Gloria told him. He nodded his head and then ran to the porch of Gibbs' house.

"How sweet, after I kill you I will kill him or maybe I'll convert him and raise him as my son," one of Dracula's brides said to Gloria. A.J. and Monica pulled out their knives, while Gloria pulled out her small dagger. "Be careful with that, it's pretty sharp, wouldn't want you to hurt yourself with that bitch."

"Don't worry, you're the only person who's gonna get hurt tonight." She hissed at Gloria and then lunged at her, causing Gloria to fall to the ground as A.J. and Monica fought the other two.

"Ha, ha, ha, ha, ha, ha," she laughed as she flew over Gloria. When Gloria got up Dracula's bride landed. "So you still wanna play?" Gloria grabbed the dagger.

"Oh fun time hasn't even started yet." She swung at the bride, but did not hit her. She continued to miss making contact with Dracula's bride, every time she swung at her she moved away.

"This is pointless, let me finish you now," Dracula's bride said to Gloria. She grabbed Gloria's hands and flipped her over her head. Gloria was almost stabbed by her own dagger on the way down. The dagger was to the right of her shoulder, as her face lay in the grass. She turned herself over only to see Dracula's bride force her body on her. "Ha, ha, ha, I'm gonna enjoy this." She hissed as her face got closer to Gloria's neck. She moved so close to her neck, Gloria could feel her neck tickle. Gloria grabbed the dagger with her left hand and put it through Dracula's bride's heart. "Ahhhhhhhh!" Dracula's bride dissolved into dust.

"Be careful with that, it's pretty sharp, wouldn't want you to hurt yourself with that bitch."

In the intervening period of time, Dracula was still trying to open his eyes after having the garlic spray showered into them. When he opened them his eye sight was blurry. He could see something white moving slowly toward him. When he was almost knocked off his feet he knew it was a punch. Tim stood him up straight and punched him again. Dracula was still seeing blurry when Travis punched him in his jaw, causing him to spit up blood. Travis tried to punch him again, but Dracula caught his fist. He looked up at Travis with an evil smile.

"No, it will not be that easy," he told Travis. He cracked Travis' knuckles, causing him to bend down to his knees, in serious pain. Tim jumped in the air and kicked Dracula in his face, he fell backwards hitting the pavement.

"You alright?" Tim asked Travis.

"Yeah," Travis responded.

"I am too," Dracula said, as he rose up from the pavement as if he had been lying in a coffin. He picked both of them up and threw them high in the air. They knew once they hit the concrete the impact would kill them. Dracula turned around hoping to see them fall to their death, instead he witnessed Frankenstein's monster catch them.

"You're free," Tim told the monster.

"Frankenstein had to save friends," the monster said as he put both of them down.

"Theodore call for help!," Dracula yelled.

"Sure," Theodore said. He turned into his werewolf form, this time standing up straight. He howled for a whole minute and after 2 minutes passed ten werewolves were there. "Kill them!"

"Frankenstein run!," the monster said. He ran towards all of the werewolves. Two of them attacked him right away. He picked both of them up and broke their necks by pulling their heads off. Tim wanted to help kill the werewolvess but Dracula was in his way. Travis and Tim saw him, but he disappeared.

"Where did he go?" Travis asked Tim.

"I don't know, I just saw him in front of us," Tim said. They ran across the street to look for him. When he reappeared he was behind Tim. The Count grabbed his hair and pushed him face first into a tree, causing him to lose consciousness. Travis turned around and was surprised to see Tim laying by the tree.

"What?" He turned around and Dracula was behind him.

"No, who," Dracula said with a smile on his face. He swung at Travis, but he was able to duck his punch. Two of the wolves went after Gibbs and Christopher while they were sitting on the porch. Gloria and A.J. were fighting one of Dracula's brides when they heard Gloria's name being called by Christopher. Dracula's bride knocked them both down.

"A.J. you're gonna have to handle this chick by yourself, I have a little boy to save," Gloria told her as she checked to see if her mouth was bleeding.

"Don't worry, I got her," A.J. said. They both got up, but went in opposite directions. Gloria ran towards the sound of Christopher's voice while A.J. stared down Dracula's bride. Dracula's bride taunted A.J., but every time A.J. would run to her she would disappear and laugh. The third time she did it she reappeared behind A.J. She grabbed A.J. by her hair and threw her down. A.J. was more upset than hurt when her face hit the grass.

"You'll never be able to get me," Dracula's bride said.

"Yeah, you're using all that magic on your side," A.J. said.

"Excuses, excuses, all you humans do is make excuses."

"I thought you were human once."

"I was, how drag, feels like a different life time."

"It's only been about 20 to 25 years."

"But it feels longer, you see I was his first bride."

"How lucky you are." A.J. tried to stab her with the knife she had, but Dracula's bride jumped into the air. When she came down out of the air she was smiling at A.J.

"After the book opened he was on that world lonely, by himself, he asked me if I wanted to live forever. I told him that's impossible, everyone dies. He said if you marry me I will make you mine forever. I accepted and he bit me on the spot. It hurt a little I admit, but I'm happy he did it now that I have eternal life."

"Eternal life until I kill you and send you to hell!" A.J. cut her with the knife, drawing blood. She tried to cut Dracula's bride again, but she pushed A.J.'s head, pushing her back, almost causing her to fall. She had a serious look on her face as she followed A.J. Two police cars pulled up. Dracula's bride looked at the two cars and smiled.

"Good more food, after I'm done with you."

"Everyone freeze!," one of the four cops said. They were startled when one of the brides appeared behind them. The officers stood in shock.

"Are you sure you want me to freeze officer, I can dance," one of Dracula's brides said. When she saw one of the officers looked very young she made her way to him. She began dancing sexy, which caused the young officer's heart to beat faster. She rubbed him on his cheek and kissed him. "I can also bite." She bit the young officer on his neck. His partner tried to run, but was greeted by Dracula.

"Leaving so soon?" Dracula asked the officer. He hissed at him and then bit him in his neck.

"Ahhhhhhh!," the officer screamed. The last two cops tried to shoot at Dracula's bride, but the bullets didn't affect her. She walked up to one of them and bit him on his neck.

"Marguerite," Dracula's bride said, calling the vampire who was fighting A.J. Marguerite looked up at her. "I'm saving this one for you."

"Wrong, I'm saving this one for you!," Monica said, as she

put the knife through the vampire's heart.

"Ahhhhhh!," she screamed.

"No!," Dracula screamed. Marguerite was in shock as she saw her sister dissolve. She wanted to take her anger out on A.J., but she was gone. Monica became scared when she heard Dracula's voice, hence she ran as Dracula's bride dissolved into dust. Dracula threw the cop down and went after Monica. The last officer got back in his car and drove off in fear.

"Where did she go?" Marguerite, Dracula's first bride asked. "When I find that girl...., come out where ever you are!" A.J. fell from the tree above her and let go of the knife on the way down. Her knife went directly into Marguerite's heart. "Ahhhhhhh!"

"You're not the only one with magic tricks," A.J. said as she dissolved into dust. Michael ran over to A.J. and hugged her.

"Man I'm glad you're o.k.," Michael said.

"Yeah I am, watch out!" A werewolf jumped on to Michael's back, causing him to fall face first into the grass. The werewolf was drooling as it prepared to eat him. A.J. stood there in fear, helpless, unable to do or say anything. Frankenstein's monster grabbed the werewolf and bashed its head into the ground, splattering it. Michael's heart beat was racing fast.

"Thanks big fella, I owe you one, that was close." A.J. had tears running down her face as she squatted down to put his head in her arms.

"Michael safe now," the monster said.

"Yes, Michael is safe now."

Meanwhile Gloria confronted the two werewolves who were trying to attack Christopher and Gibbs.

"Hey!," Gloria yelled in order to take the focus off of Gibbs and Christopher. They turned around and chased after her. She realized she didn't have a plan after getting their attention. Benji came to her rescue with his machete and struck both werewolves with it. They were bleeding nonstop after being hit with the machete several times, hence they ran away. Unfortunately Mark was attacked by two of them. They bit through his skin before Benji arrived and began hitting them with the machete. When Tim woke up he heard screaming. He got the gun he purchased from Edwin and fired at every werewolf he saw, killing three as they tried to run away from Benji. Three more werewolves were ready to kill Edward when Tim shot all of them with silver bullets. The last werewolf, which was Theodore, knocked him off his feet before he could shoot him. He was on the verge of killing Tim when Frankenstein's monster picked him up by his tail, spun him around like he was a merry-go-round and slammed him to the ground. Theodore got back up and bit the monster's hand.

"Ahhhhhh!," Frankenstein's monster said.

"Finish this trader off," Dracula said. No one could get close enough to them without them seeing it first. Tim reached for his gun, but was grabbed by Dracula, who put him in a head lock. "You know how easy it would be for me to break your neck right now?" Tim tried to get free, with very little success. "Don't even go for the garlic, cause if you keep moving I will break your neck." A.J., Gloria and Benji tried to run up on him. "Stay where you are, all of you or I will kill your fearless leader." That stopped everyone from moving. Dracula noticed someone was missing. He looked around trying to figure out who it was. He saw Travis in front of him, Benji was with Gloria, Michael with A.J., he knew Mark was almost dead and that Monica was probably with him and, he saw Gibbs and Christopher on the porch of the house.

"Looking for me?" Edward asked. He was holding the bow and arrow with silver darts he found the night before in Dracula's weapon room. While Dracula's head was turned Tim elbowed him in his chest, causing his grip to loosen as the silver that Edward fired came at him. "This is for Mark!" The silver dart went half way through his heart, causing Dracula to breathe hard. His face showed disbelief and shock. "All those weapons in the weapons room, they were not for your protection, they were weapons you got from people you killed, like the cannibals. That's why some of the weapons there were dangerous to you, all those clothes were from people you killed. A.J. was suspicious, but we all should've seen it." Dracula still had a look of shock on his face. A.J. ran up to him and kicked the silver arrow all the way through his body.

"Ahhhhhhhhh!" As he was dissolving Theodore tried to sneak away, but was apprehended by Frankenstein's monster, who picked him up with one hand as if he were a little kid.

"What are you gonna do?" Theodore asked all of the visitors from a parallel dimension. He looked at Tim as he pulled out his gun. "You ain't got what it takes to do it, you're a coward." Tim shot him and when the silver bullets went through him Frankenstein's monster let go of his dead body.

"I guess I do have what it takes," Tim said.

CHAPTER 15

Tim ran over to Mark, where Monica was crying.

"Make sure you get to the time machine," Mark told her as he was breathing hard. She continued to cry. When Mark stopped breathing Tim checked his pulse.

"He's dead," Tim said.

"No!," Monica cried.

"Travis." Travis came and pulled her away from his dead body.

"Gibbs is he gonna turn, he was bit by a werewolf and a zombie," Tim said.

"I don't think so, but to be on the safe side burn his body," Gibbs said as some of them got in the pickup truck.

"Travis!" Travis turned around. "Lighter."

"No!," Monica cried.

"It'll be alright," Gloria told her as she helped her into the pickup truck. "Don't watch." Gloria put her hands over Monica's eyes as they sat on the back of the pickup truck together. Monica put her head on Gloria's lap as she continued to cry. Christopher, who was now asleep, lay on Michael's lap.

"We may still need the big guy," Tim told Travis.

"Yeah, I think so," Travis said as they watched the fire burn.

Professor Gibbs was looking out of his window as he saw K.B.G.'s run over citizens on his street. He went into the basement and turned on the dimensional machine.

"Well time to go to another dimension, nothing can be this bad," Professor Gibbs said. He was about to press the button to type in a destination when his wall caved through. He was surprised to see Frankenstein's monster standing in front of him. He tried to run up the stairs, but was thrown off the first two steps by Travis. Edward, Tim, Benji, Michael, A.J., Gloria, Monica, Christopher, and Gibbs were behind him. "You, you, what are you doing here, how did you get back here, how did those monsters get here?" He looked at all of them and was surprised to see Gibbs. "You."

"Yes me, the man you left stranded on the nightmare world," Gibbs said. "You visited this world by accident." He looked at all of his new friends. "He had no way of returning, he wasn't like me, he didn't know how to get back to his world, but he made sure I wouldn't be able to get back here, but I did with the help of all of you." He looked at Professor Gibbs. "You left me to die."

"It was a mistake, what are you gonna do with me, I told you it was a mistake." Tim lifted him up by his shirt.

"A mistake, you see what's going on, because of you now those monsters followed us from the nightmare world here." Tim threw Professor Gibb's to the floor.

"But I had to escape from the nightmare world, I hated it, that's the real reason I sent all of you there. Halloween reminded me too much of the old world I used to stay in."

"And now this world is the nightmare world," Benji said. "The nightmare world is completely uninhabited."

"We should send you there where you'll be lonely forever," Tim said.

"No," Professor Gibbs said.

"Frankenstein hold him."

"Frankenstein hold Professor Gibbs," the monster said as he picked him off of the ground and held on to his arm.

"So what's the plan Gibbs, or should I say Professor Gibbs?" Benji asked Gibbs.

"Yeah, I think you deserve to be called Professor Gibbs instead of this cowardly loser," Travis told him.

"I still haven't gotten things back the way they were," Gibbs said. "How did you get this house anyway?"

"Did you kill someone to get it?" Edward asked Professor Gibbs.

"No, I have been working for the government, sharing a few viruses here and there I collected on the nightmare world, they gave me this house, but promised more if I shared my secrets," Professor Gibbs explained.

"Instead of using this machine for peace and love you wanted to use it for destruction and chaos," Gibbs told himself.

"Well what else?" A.J. rolled her eyes.

"The real Professor Gibbs was traveling different worlds looking for a cure for cancer," Tim said.

"I never thought of that."

"I'm sure you didn't."

"We have to get started, we are running out of time, as long as he didn't mess with the time machine it should still work," Gibbs said. He turned on the time machine. "What time did the last person get captured?" He looked at his other self. "What time?" Frankenstein's monster began choking him. Professor Gibbs waved his arms so the monster would stop. Once his hands were off his neck he began talking fast.

"Alright, alright, about 9:26 pm," Professor Gibbs told his other self.

"We'll send you guys back about 9:19, directly in the back of the Professor's house."

"But Professor Gibbs, aren't you coming with us?" A.J. asked.

"No honey, there's no need for me to come."

"But we need you," Travis said.

"Yeah," the others agreed.

"You will succeed without me, I believe in all of you," Gibbs told them.

"If we do succeed it's gonna be at a bad cost," Gloria said.

"What do you mean?" Edward asked her.

"I don't know if I'm right Professor Gibbs, but if I am tell them before we do this, so they can all know"

"What is it Professor Gibbs?" Michael asked. Gibbs took a deep breath before talking.

"My friends if you go back in time and stop this other Professor Gibbs from sending you to the nightmare world, all of the things that you did the last few days, all that's happened, would be erased from time."

"What are you saying?" Edward asked.

"It would be like none of it happened."

"Including rescuing you from Homicidal Asylum," Tim said. Gibbs nodded his head while the room got quiet.

"You were in there for two years, if we reset history and we're not there to save you, who knows how long you will be there," A.J. said, getting emotional.

"It's o.k. A.J.," Gibbs said before hugging her as a few tears rolled down her face. "This is my home and I won't let it be destroyed, I will be happier in that asylum knowing my world is safe instead of seeing my world destroyed. That will happen if you don't go back in time." He set the time machine. "Now who's going?"

"I thought we all had to go," Gloria said.

"No, whoever stays will wake up in the Professor's cage, you will remember none of this."

"So it'll be like we never left?"

"Yes my dear."

"Count me and Christopher to stay, I don't mind forgetting this." Benji looked down at Professor Gibbs' floor. He was afraid Gloria would forget about their time together. "Oh Benji I won't forget about you, I promise." She kissed Benji on his lips as Christopher smiled.

"So what's gonna happen to the people that do go?" Tim asked.

"You will remember everything," Gibbs said.

"What's gonna happen when we succeed?" Michael asked.

"The second you succeed you will be placed in a time warp."

"A time warp?" Benji asked.

"Yes, you will see a huge flash of light or you will see time itself freeze and then move in slow motion. Whenever the time warp is over you will be back where you started from."

"In the cages," Tim said.

"Yes."

"Well I'm going, T Money?"

"As usual, I'm going," Travis said.

"Mark told me to go, so I'm gonna honor his last words before he died," Monica said.

"Don't worry, you'll see him again," Gibbs assured her.

Edward, Benji, Michael and A.J. agreed to go. Gibbs gave them all hoodies to wear. "Remember the plan and keep your face down, you don't wanna send your other self in to shock by seeing you."

"Frankenstein will miss friends," the monster said.

"We'll miss you too Frankie," A.J. said.

"Bye big guy, thanks," Michael told him. They saw Gibbs press a button on the time machine and in a flash they were gone. When they reappeared they were outside of Professor Gibbs' house. Monica heard something that she wanted to see.

"Monica where are you going?" Tim asked her in a whispering voice. She got close to the front, but stayed hidden. She could see herself with Mark, walking towards Professor Gibbs' house. She turned to Tim, who was on the side of her watching in the bush.

"It's like watching a movie," Monica told Tim quietly. Tim smiled at her. After Mark and Monica are captured, Professor Gibbs went downstairs to the cages with an evil smile on his face.

"It's done, it's done!," he said.

"Where are we?" Monica asked.

"Don't worry about it, cause now I'm sending you somewhere else!" When he tried to press the button on the machine the power in the house went out causing the kids to scream. "What happened, I must've blown a fuse, I'll be back kids." He walked up the stairs, but returned quickly. He was holding a candle in his hand when the power came back on. "I wonder what happened." When he walked back to the machine he pressed the button in order to transport the kids in the cages to the nightmare world. "Have fun kids, ha, ha, ha, ha." He was fearful of his fate when he felt his body moving. "What's this, what's happening?" Tim and the others came out of hiding and showed themselves to Professor Gibbs.

"We set a new heading for your machine," Tim said.

"Impossible, impossible!"

"You didn't know it ran on backup power, but oh yeah, that's cause you didn't invent this, the other Professor Gibbs did, now you will be joining him in the nightmare world."

"No, I can't go back there, I can't go back there, I can't go back there, Noooooooo!" All of the kids in the cages were amazed when they saw him disappear. The time travelers had headaches, causing them to fall to the floor. A flash of lightning struck Professor Gibbs' house. The lightning lit up the sky for 2 minutes. In those 2 minutes the time travelers saw themselves moving in slow motion. Once the flash disappeared they found themselves waking up with the rest of the kids in the cages.

"We're back," Benji said.

"Back, we never went anywhere," Gloria said.

"Easy for you to say," Edward said.

"What is that supposed to mean?"

"You don't' wanna know," Tim said.

"Well how do you know I don't wanna know storm trooper, you don't even know me."

"I know you better than you think I do Gloria." He winked at her which caused Gloria to make an ugly expression appear on her face. Benji laughed at her reaction.

"Oh my goodness Benji, he knows my name." Benji continued to laugh.

"Mark I'm glad you're o.k.," Monica told Mark.

"Why wouldn't I be Monica?" Mark asked.

"Nothing, I'm just happy to see you." She hugged him.

Outside two squad cars pulled up.

"We're responding to the disturbance outside of 232 Linden Avenue," one of the officers said on his walkie-talkie. Four officers came in the house, when they reached the basement the kids cheered. The police officers smiled and then began opening the cages with whatever they could find. Gloria kissed Benji on the cheek.

"What was that for?" Benji asked.

"I don't know, I feel like you deserve it for some reason, strange huh?" Gloria asked.

"Yeah." Benji smiled.

"A.J. do you remember?" Michael asked.

"Everything," A.J. said before kissing Michael on the lips. The police officers opened their cage and they got out.

"Someone better tell me what happened here," one of the officers said. Tim looked at the officer with his friends behind him.

"So talk."

"Are you sure?" Tim asked.

"Yeah."

"Well you're gonna need a few notebooks to take down all what I'm about to tell you." Tim and his friends laughed.